Dina
5/1/89

A Killer Without a Conscience!

Ned casually laid his rifle down on the table, turned his back on the nester, and walked over to the cupboards. He opened one of the cabinets and reached up for a can of beans. He heard the nester behind him lunge toward him.

Pulling his six-gun, Ned whirled and fired. The muzzle of his revolver was only inches from the nester's chest. The slug punched a neat hole in his dirty nightshirt and exploded out of his back, spraying blood over the chair Ned had just left. With the barrel of his six-gun, Ned slammed the dazed man on the head and drove him to his knees.

As he collapsed facedown onto the floor, Ned heard the nester's wife sob and cry out. . . .

x

LONGARM AND THE MAD DOG KILLER

A Jove Book/published by arrangement with
the author

PRINTING HISTORY
Jove edition/April 1989

ISBN: 0-515-09985-6

Jove Books are published by The Berkley Publishing Group
200 Madison Avenue, New York, New York 10016.
The name "JOVE" and the "J" logo
are trademarks belonging to Jove Publications, Inc.

PRINTED IN THE UNITED STATES OF AMERICA

10 9 8 7 6 5 4 3 2 1

Prologue

Ned Larson felt the eyes of the other passengers on him. He didn't care. Let them look. They would not soon see his like pass their way again. It gave him a fierce, perverse joy to contemplate the awe—and the fear—in their faces when they watched him nudged, handcuffed, down the aisle to his seat.

He glanced out the window. Hills dipped swiftly, rose, dipped again. Snowcapped peaks gleamed in the distance. Blue sky. Telegraph poles stroked past the windows. Under his seat came the steady click of the wheels passing over the rail sections. He heard the chuff and wail of the steam engine up ahead. Behind him in the coach a brat was crying.

Across from him sat the deputy U.S. marshal. Tom Crane. Clean shaven, his eyes peering out at him from under gentle, sandy eyebrows. Ned had already caught the softness under the U.S. marshal's tough exterior. The poor stupid son of a bitch had been reluctant, even apologetic at having to bring Ned onto the train in handcuffs.

And once on the train the lawman should have cuffed his own left hand to Ned's right and sat beside him, crowding him to the inside. Instead, he had cuffed Ned's hands together and made sure that Ned had a seat to himself. All this revealed to Ned more than softness. It was a slack, girlish weakness. A spineless compassion.

Ned watched Tom Crane carefully through slitted eyes. He noted the exhausted marshal's slack face, his heavy lids. The man was almost asleep. Something deeply subterranean in Ned Larson smiled. Laughter shook his dark soul, and he felt strength building within him. An invincible strength, more than enough to enable him to take this soft fool of a marshal.

Ned Larson's strength came from his certainty that he had no soul. That *no one* had a soul. That all men were no more fortunate than the beasts of the field, the fowl of the air, the fish of the sea. This certainty meant that he, like all men, was a creature without an afterworld to look forward to or a deity to guide him. And just as man could kill the soulless creatures about him without concern, so man could kill his own kind with as little compunction. If men were without souls, it did not matter what they did to each other, just as it did not matter how many deer he shot, how many bear or buffalo he brought down. Or birds he shot out of the sky. One could kill or debase without concern and without end. For there were no consequences, not any that mattered. The truth of it was that nothing mattered. Nothing. *Nada*.

It was Ned's father who taught Ned this awesome, powerful secret.

A Lutheran minister, Reverend Larson was a violent and cruel master. He drank himself into towering rages, beat his wife and Ned with metronomic regularity, and satisfied his bestial lusts with his own daughter. It was when Ned confronted his father while he was still crouched, naked, over Ned's sister that the reverend had imparted his secret to Ned, doing so with such drunken, blasphemous eloquence that Ned was completely convinced.

Ned had no soul. There was no God. No waiting hellfire. Nothing.

Ned promptly beat his father's head to jelly with the blade of a shovel and fled Minnesota, setting his face west. For some reason he could not entirely explain, his secret knowledge of the futility of all human endeavor gave him a singular advantage—one that he soon learned to exploit with great skill. He would continue to do so until he found at last the only thing he truly wanted: a quick and sudden descent into the oblivion that awaited all living creatures.

Ned hoped it would come for him in the guise of a bullet through his brain. He had come close to nothingness, but always, for one reason or another, he had escaped. His reckless disregard for his own life and those of others tended to freeze men into impotence. They pissed in their pants and backed down. While others simply refused to believe that this smiling, blue-eyed young outlaw could possibly be as bad as claimed.

The train lifted under him as it began to ascend a steep grade. He glanced out the window. Beyond the flashing telegraph poles the ground fell away rapidly. It was time. Abruptly he held out his manacled wrists, thrusting them close under Tom Crane's chin. The marshal came alert and pulled back, blinking in surprise.

"What's this, Ned?"

"These here manacles are damned heavy. Get 'em off, will you, Tom?"

Crane shook his head. "Against regulations."

"The hell with regulations. My wrists are raw. Where the hell could I go? I'm on a train. You got sharp eyes and a loaded revolver. I won't pull nothin'. Hell, I ain't crazy. . . . Besides, I need to pee, Tom. With these damn chains on, I get myself wet all down my front." He grinned suddenly at the U.S. marshal. "You want to sit across from a man smellin' of fresh piss?"

Tom stirred reluctantly, then shrugged. "I'll take 'em off, then escort you down to the toilet. When you come out, they go back on."

"Fair enough, Tom. And I sure do appreciate it."

Ned's smile was disarming, shy almost. Tom fished the key out of his side pocket, unlocked the cuffs and then, drawing his Colt, left his seat and stood up. Ned pushed himself gratefully upright and proceeded ahead of Tom down the

4

aisle, past the staring faces. Two settlers' kids, all eyes and freckles, turned in their seats to follow him as he passed. The sight of the enormous Colt Peacemaker in Crane's hand hushed them instantly.

Inside the toilet Ned buttoned his fly, turned about in the narrow compartment, and pushed open the door. He turned his back on Tom to close the door. He felt the man's presence behind him and rammed himself suddenly back, twisting around as he did so. He plunged his elbow deep into Tom's gut. The lawman's breath exploded from his lungs. He dropped the Colt. Ned snatched it up and clubbed Tom repeatedly over the head with it, grunting with the exertion of each blow. He kept at it until the lawman hit the floor and the Colt's heavy barrel had broken through Tom's skull, turning his hair and the top of his skull into a bloody, bone-flecked soup.

He stood up. He had acted so swiftly that two passengers only now were turning in their seats to see what the commotion was. One of them was a fat, doughy-faced drummer, the other an old cowpoke. Ned caught their eyes. His hard, wild gleam stopped them. Both men flinched back.

"That's it," Ned said softly, waggling the gun at them. "Just lean back in your seats and there won't be no trouble."

The two men did so. Others turned their heads, frowning. Ned pulled the emergency cord. Instantly the coach slowed, throwing everyone forward in their seats. From under

Ned's feet came a grinding screech as the steel wheels locked and skidded along the flanged rails. A woman screamed. A baby started to cry. The conductor burst through the door. Ned buried the muzzle of the Colt in the man's midsection and pulled the trigger. The detonation was partially muffled by the conductor's body. Carrying Ned's gun with him, the man crashed heavily to the floor farther down the aisle. Ned stepped toward the platform. The train was slowing rapidly. Swinging open the door, Ned flung himself out.

The ground rushed up at him. He hit the steep incline and sprawled forward. Cinders dug into his knees as he rolled down the embankment. He came to a halt in a clump of grass, stood up and saw the train squealing to a halt about two hundred yards farther up the grade.

Turning his back on it, he ran off, heading toward a cluster of low-lying hills.

Ned peered at the horse inside the corral. He shook his head. The horse was no better than a nag. Sorrowful. Pitiful. It would not take him more than a mile, if that far. But it would have to do. He was footsore and weary.

A door slammed shut. The sound came from behind the nester's shack. He ducked low. A woman emerged from around the corner. She was lugging a wooden bucket, heading for the well. She would have to pass right by him and could not fail to see him when she did.

Ned crouched lower.

It took a surprisingly long time for her to glance over and see him crouching in the grass beside the corral. When she did, she was less than ten feet away. She dropped the bucket and recoiled as he sprang toward her and uttered a short, inarticulate cry. Catching her about the neck, he dragged her to the ground beside him. He heard someone come running in heavy clodhoppers from the barn. With a series of quick chopping blows to the side of the neck, he knocked the woman senseless, then leaped to his feet and dashed to meet whomever it was coming from the barn. Breaking from around the corner of the shack, he found himself only a few feet from the nester. The big dumb son of a bitch was carrying only a pitchfork.

Ned launched himself at the astonished nester. The man was bigger and heftier about the shoulders than Ned. But Ned struck him with such speed, multiplied by the element of surprise, that the farmer went reeling backward, dropping his pitchfork as he did so. Ned landed on the man's big chest, and slamming his elbow down with all his force, crushed the farmer's windpipe. It sounded like a dry twig snapping underfoot. The nester gurgled and coughed up some blood, then lay still.

Ned went back to the woman. She was still unconscious, but very much alive. There was even a faint, rosy flush to her face. She was waiting for him. Chuckling, he unbuckled his pants swiftly and straddled her. As he entered her, she came awake and screamed. He tried to pin her arms. She would not let him. He hit her on the point of her chin. Again. Again. And again. Her screams ceased abruptly. He reached down and cupped her chin in his palm and shook her head. It felt as if it were no longer attached to her spinal column. One of the blows must have broken her neck.

With a shrug, he finished what he had started.

The horse was done. Its muzzle flecked with dried foam, eyes starting from its head, it had given up at last and sagged to the ground. Ned looked down at it and waited. Gamely, the animal tried to struggle upright. Ned kicked it about the neck and head. The horse threw itself about frantically in an effort to push itself upright and almost made it. Then it sagged back onto the ground, ragged flags of foam billowing from its muzzle as it wheezed desperately. Ned kicked it a couple more times, then slung the saddlebags over his shoulder and moved off, heading on through the trees.

The horse had carried him a good distance into the hills. More than he had thought possible when he saddled him up and rode out, the nester's big old Navy Colt and holster strapped to his thigh. There had been fresh food in the shack, but he had taken only the canned beans and sardines, stuffing them along with a few other items he would need into the saddlebags he had confiscated along with the saddle.

The saddlebags now heavy on his shoulder, an hour or so later he caught the gleam of water through the trees ahead. He kept going and halted just inside the timber at the edge of a clearing bordered by a broad mountain stream. A towheaded cowpoke was squatting in the stream's shallows, filling his hat with water. His horse—a good-looking chestnut saddle horse— was craning its neck eagerly. It was anxious for the water. Ned drew his Navy Colt and stepped out of the timber.

The cowboy stood up with his hat full of water, turned, and saw Ned advancing.

Ned grinned. The cowpoke dropped the hat and slapped for his side arm. Ned raised his Colt calmly and fired. The first bullet caught the cowpoke in the gut, doubling him over. The second one dug up the ground beside him. The third took off the top of his head.

The three quick detonations caused the horse to bolt off down the stream. Ned walked after it, gentling it patiently with a soft, almost wheedling tone. The horse pulled up, lifted its head nervously. Trembling from head to toe, it watched Ned for a moment. Ned kept on coming, still talking patiently, his tone soothing. The horse's tail dropped. It's ears stopped flickering.

Abruptly it turned and headed on a light trot for the stream bank. Ned increased his pace. He didn't want the horse to drink too much.

This was a fine animal. Not your usual cow pony. It could take him far.

Chapter 1

Glancing up from his hand—a good one: full house, king high—Longarm saw Billy Vail entering the Windsor Hotel bar. When the U.S. marshal caught sight of Longarm, he headed directly for his table. The intent look on Billy Vail's face alerted Longarm.

"I'm out," Longarm told the dealer, folding his hand and pushing his chair back.

"What's up, Billy?" Longarm asked, meeting the U.S. marshal halfway across the floor.

"I want a drink first."

The two men found an empty booth. The bartender hurried over and took their order. When Vail's drink arrived, he took a healthy belt, then leaned back in his seat and looked wearily at Longarm.

"I just got a telegram. Tom Crane's dead."

This news shook Longarm. Before he went to work for Vail, Longarm had cut a few trails with Tom Crane, and it was on Longarm's recommendation a few months ago that Vail had hired Tom. Since both operatives were usually off on different assignments, they had had damn few opportunities to raise a glass in greeting.

Now there would be no more such opportunities.

"What happened, Billy?"

"It was a long enough telegram. Told the whole story. Came from the Lewistown sheriff in Montana. Seems Larson broke loose on the train, killed Tom and a conductor, then lit out across country. On his way he managed to rape and kill a settler's wife, then for good measure, killed the settler. Later, he came on a cowpoke, shot him down, and took his horse. I figure he might be heading for the border right now."

"He'll be long gone, then."

"Maybe not. I wired Foster at Fort Macleod. Them mounties will be looking for him the moment he crosses over into Alberta—if they can get loose of them Métis. I understand Louis Riel's back and stirring up more trouble."

"You want me to go after Larson?"

"Yes. I want that mad dog, Longarm—and I want him alive."

"From the sound of it, that won't be easy. Hell, Billy, what does it matter how I bring in the son of a bitch?"

"It matters because he's a witness we want, the only survivor of a botched robbery."

"Which one?"

"That attempt last year to hold up the silver shipment from the Pueblo smelter to the mint here. The silver was coming by rail under guard in a sealed coach when the gang tried to take it. The only way they could have known which car was carrying the shipment was through an informant. Someone who works in the smelter, we figure. This fellow Ned Larson could give us a lead on who it is."

Longarm remembered now. The attempt to rob the shipment had been botched from the first, every gang member either cut down by the guard or by the gang members themselves as they slung lead wildly in a frantic effort to extricate themselves. He had heard that only one of them had escaped. And this Ned Larson was that one. He was a survivor of disasters, then. Or so it appeared.

"You got a description of Larson?"

Billy Vail reached into an inside pocket and took out a thick envelope. "His description's in here, along with your travel vouchers and tickets. I want you to leave on the seven o'clock train." He pushed the envelope across the table to Longarm. "Ned looks like a nice young fellow, fresh out from behind his mother's apron strings. He couldn't be more than twenty-two or three, has a mop of sandy hair and is all blue eyes and smiles—to the right person. But watch him. He's a killer."

"You called him a mad dog."

"If you don't believe me, ask Sheriff Stallings. You'll find him in Lewistown. You know the country?"

Longarm nodded. He knew Lewistown. It

was the seat of Fergus County, deep in the big-sky country. Montana was a territory still, but there was talk of statehood. With the buffalo gone and the Sioux and Crow locked up in their agencies, it was mostly cow country now, with a few brazen sheepmen edging in. Wide-open spaces. A lot of running room for a killer like Ned Larson.

"What's the sheriff's name, Billy?"

"John Stallings. A good man, I hear, but he's not very happy about now—not with four dead citizens on his hands. And that ain't including Tom. It sure as hell don't make him look good."

"Now ain't that just too goddamned bad."

Billy held up his hand. "Now, don't get your dander up, Long. I'm only telling it like it is. Stallings has a right to be unhappy. He apprehended Ned Larson and handed him over to Tom. He did his part. Just get up there and get that little son of a bitch for me. Bring Larson back alive. That's all I ask."

"Is that all, Billy?"

"Dammit, Long, don't push me. It's been a long day."

Longarm pulled his drink closer, then tipped it quickly down his gullet. Sure. He would bring Ned Larson back in leg irons and handcuffs—if he could manage it. Otherwise, he'd lace Larson's body with hot lead and take whatever heat Billy Vail dished out.

The important thing was to get the bastard.

• • •

14

It was noon on the next day when Longarm reached Lewistown. After he stashed his McClellan, Winchester, bedroll and possibles in his hotel room, he went in search of Sheriff Stallings. He found the sheriff in his office in the county jail. It was a two-story frame building fronting a broad avenue within sight of the train depot.

Entering the sheriff's office, Longarm shucked his hat back off his head and nodded to the man busy at his rolltop desk. The sheriff appeared to be filing a dodger. He glanced up curtly at Longarm's entrance. Longarm towered in the small room. Better than six feet in height, he was a man who tended to spook cattle if he moved too quickly out of the shadows. He had been known to spook gunslicks the same way. Longarm halted in front of the desk.

"Sheriff Stallings?"

"That's me," the sheriff said, swiveling around in his chair to get a better look at Longarm. The man was chunky in build, a good deal shorter than Longarm, with jet-black hair and powerful beetling brows. His eyes were anthracite, as well. His Indian blood fitted well with that part of him that was white, however, and there was a rugged honesty in his face that Longarm found difficult not to like.

"I'm U.S. Deputy Marshal Long," he said, opening his wallet and flashing his badge.

The sheriff did not bother to glance at it. "I

know who you are, Deputy. Saw you get off the train. Welcome to Lewistown."

The sheriff's welcome belied his manner. It was obvious he was weary with the events of the past week and not a bit happy at having to deal with another U.S. marshal from Denver. He hadn't had much luck with the last one. Longarm caught his weary exasperation and decided not to resent it.

"I'm up here after Ned Larson," Longarm said. "I'd appreciate any help you could give me, Sheriff."

"I'll bet you would."

"Mind if I sit down?"

"Pull up a chair."

Stallings pulled a clay pipe out of his side pocket and began thumbing fresh tobacco into the bowl. Longarm lifted a chair away from the wall and brought it over to the desk. Slumping into it, he took out a cheroot. A moment later, as both men sat back in clouds of fragrant smoke, the sheriff regained his civility.

"I suppose you knew that deputy Larson killed," he said.

"I knew him and I liked him. He was a good friend. Had been for a long way back."

The sheriff's eyes grew somber. "Guess that means you've got a damned good incentive for collaring Larson."

"Trouble is, my orders are to take the bastard alive. He's a witness to a bungled heist."

"Yeah. Tom Crane told me about it."

16

"Just how'd it happen, Sheriff? Tom Crane was no fool."

"No offense intended, Long, but maybe this time he was. Larson was in cuffs and leg irons when I took him out of his cell. But Tom allowed Larson to get on the train wearing only handcuffs."

"No leg irons, you say?"

"No. And from the witnesses' accounts, the handcuffs were off Larson when Crane took him back to use the toilet."

"How do you figure all this?"

"Ned Larson. It's the look of him."

"What do you mean?"

"He's a baby face. Ain't much past twenty, I'd say. Thing is, he don't *look* dangerous. Looks like someone left his Sunday-school choir. Of course he couldn't keep it up. When he was in that cell back there, I could feel his eyes on me—they burnt on my neck like coals out of hell. Then I'd glance over at him, quick like, just to catch him. And he'd smile at me and you wouldn't want for a nicer, cleaner lookin' young man. But he's got a black heart, that one. Only most of the time he keeps it well hidden. Until he strikes."

"Like with Tom Crane."

"Guess that's the size of it."

"How'd you manage to collar him in the first place?"

"He was stayin' with a widow on her ranch out of town. Stella Rooney. The Lazy J. He went crazy or something, near beat her to death. She bided her time, and when she was well enough, she rode in and visited me. He'd done some talking, so she knew he was wanted. Next time she came in, she brought him with her, and I was waiting."

"Neat."

"He'd beat up on the wrong lady when he turned on Stella Rooney."

"I'd like to meet her. Maybe she could give me a line on where Larson might be heading."

"Maybe she could at that. But right now she's a very nervous woman. When she turned Larson in, he made it pretty clear what he would do to her if he ever got free. His threat made my hair curl—because I knew he meant every word of it."

"Does it seem likely he'd double back here?"

"No, it don't. But nothing about this killer seems likely, if you know what I mean."

"How far out of town did the train get before he escaped?"

"Not far. About fifteen miles."

"I'd like to ride out there, get a look at his tracks if I could."

"Sure. I'll be through here before long. Get a horse at the livery, and I'll meet you there around one-thirty."

Longarm got up. "Much obliged, Sheriff."

"Call me John, I guess." He grinned suddenly, his teeth flashing in his dark face. "Guess I ain't as pissed off as I was when you walked in here. Hell, maybe you're just what I need. Some help."

"That's what I'm here for, John," Longarm said as he strode from the office.

They were at the nester's shack. A wooden water bucket lay on its side near the corral fence. Longarm set it upright, then looked around. It was a sad-looking place. Everything about the buildings and the land said hardscrabble. He could feel the effort and brute hard work that must have gone into felling the cottonwoods along the stream below, hauling the logs up here and sawing them, then disking out the sod squares and lugging them up onto the roof. They had done their best, but their best hadn't been very good. Already the roof's ridgepole was sagging, and Longarm could smell the outhouse, even though it was around in back. The poor dumb greenhorn hadn't dug his hole deep enough. None of them ever did, it seemed.

Stallings stood with his back to the corral fence.

"We found Jane Hollister sprawled on her back," he said, pointing at a stretch of ground in front of him. "She'd been raped, sure enough, and her neck was broken." Stallings turned and pointed toward the barn. "Her husband was found closer to the barn. He had his vocal cords crushed. It looked like he choked on his own blood. Not a pleasant way to die. This Larson knows a good many ways to kill."

They went to the nester's shack and stood in the doorway.

"From the look of it, Ned ransacked the place, took staples and other provisions, knocked things around some—like a bear scavenging—then lit out on the only saddle horse the couple owned. It wasn't much of a horse and he wasn't all that easy on it. He was lucky to find that cowpoke when he did."

"Where was it Ned found him?"

"Alongside a stream in the hills west of here."

"Let's go."

As they rode out of the silent yard, Longarm realized he hadn't heard the scratch or cluck of a single chicken about the place. He mentioned it to Stallings.

"Hell," Stallings said, "these two sodbusters were dirt poor, too poor for chickens. Don't forget, chickens have to be fed too."

"Maybe Larson did them a favor."

"You wouldn't think that if you'd seen them two bodies."

At once Longarm was sorry for his remark. The words had sounded stupid the moment they escaped his mouth. Life is sweet, no matter how tough it is, no matter how bad a hand you've been dealt. At least, while you were still in the game, there was a chance for a better deal.

Only, Ned Larson had dealt the two nesters out of the game. There was no hope for them now, no chance for a better hand.

• • •

Dismounting by the stream where the dead cowboy had been found, the two men walked along its bank, leading their horses, until they came to tracks in a patch of soft sand on the other side of the stream. Stallings hunkered down to study them.

"I know this horse Larson's ridin' 'cause I knew the cowpoke. Pete Jenks. A wild sort. Last I knew he was ridin' fence for Magnet, a ranch north of here. Guess he just lit a shuck. The only thing he cared about was his big powerful saddle horse. A chestnut. It can outrun any cow pony in the county."

"And that's what Ned Larson's ridin' now?"

"Yep. He sure as hell lucked out, comin' on Pete Jenks like that. Now he's got himself a fine mount, one it won't be all that easy to overtake."

The two men had seen the dead horse Larson had ridden into the ground, and Longarm had noted without comment the fact that the fleeing outlaw had not even bothered to shoot the poor dumb beast. Ned had just left the horse to thrash about for what appeared to have been a considerable time before expiring. One more reason— if any were needed—to hate the son of a bitch.

"Look here, Longarm," Stallings said, pointing. "At the right front foreleg. See that break in the shoe along the outside?"

Longarm peered carefully at the hoofprint. He probably would not have noticed the nick in the side of the horseshoe if the sheriff hadn't pointed it out to him. He felt some chagrin at his lapse, until he remembered that Stallings was part Indian.

The two followed the chestnut's tracks west toward the distant tumble of hills barely visible in the blue haze. Soon, the tracks faded and were lost completely in the thick, spongy grass that extended clear to the horizon. Doggedly, they kept on for an hour across the rolling prairie, descending into and rising out of draws deep enough to hide small towns. Over their heads the great blue dome of the sky arched. Every now and then Longarm searched the heavens for a cloud—and found nothing. The blue vault was as pristine and clear of flaw as blown glass. Under their mounts' hooves the ground remained thick and lush with shortgrass, buffalo and grama mostly, mixed in with clumps of bright, kelly green soap weed that grew in thick clumps along the crests of hillocks. A welcome contrast to the monotonous sweep of sun-cured grassland on all sides.

The two riders reached a welcome stream. Dismounting, they led their mounts into the cool shade of the cottonwoods lining it. They watered their weary mounts, then drank deeply of the clear water themselves, after which they sat with their backs to a cottonwood. Longarm took out a cheroot and Stallings his pipe.

"By the way," Stallings said, "mind telling me what you've got in that watch fob pocket?"

"Why, that's just my watch fob," Longarm

told him, fingering the gold-washed chain draped across his vest.

"Like hell it is. That's a belly gun you got in there."

Longarm laughed and lifted the derringer and the watch fob out of his watch pocket and handed them to the sheriff. Stallings examined the double-barreled derringer intently, his black eyes gleaming.

"This here's a .44 caliber," he noted, hefting the weapon in his palm. He smiled at Longarm as he handed the derringer back to him. "Could turn out to be a real nasty surprise for someone."

"That's the point," Longarm told him.

He slipped the watch and the derringer back into his vest pockets and went back to his cheroot.

As soon as they finished their smokes, they mounted up and spurred on across the stream, still heading west. It was Longarm who saw the sign first, tracks left by a single mount crossing a small seep. The hooves had sunk in deep, leaving neat, clear prints. They pulled up and dismounted to study them more closely.

"There," said Stallings quietly, pointing.

Longarm had seen it too—the small nick along the outside of the horse's shoe. They followed Ned's sign on foot for a few hundred yards farther on, then saw the tracks dig suddenly into the soft ground as the chestnut was turned suddenly and booted due north. The men looked at each other. Neither had to be told what this meant. Ned Larson was no longer making a beeline for the mountains to the west. He was heading for Lewistown or the border.

Or for Stella Rooney's Lazy J spread to make good on that threat.

Chapter 2

Longarm came in sight of Stella Rooney's
Lazy J an hour after leaving Lewistown. He had
set out for it as soon as he had returned to town
with the sheriff. The sun was now low on the
horizon. Its bright red eye caused him to pull his
hat brim down hastily as he crested the last ridge
and set his horse down the long grassy slope
leading to the Lazy J's ranch buildings.

As he approached the compound, an old
Mexican in an ancient sombrero and an ancient
Sharps rifle moved warily out of the horse barn
and walked over to a spot beside the gate. As
Longarm rode close, the old man lifted his rifle a
notch and let loose with a gob of tobacco juice.
His drooping handlebar mustache was already
stained amber.

On the other side of the compound, a
scrawny redhead not much older than twenty
appeared and took a position in the bunkhouse
doorway. The kid crossed his arms and leaned
back against the doorjamb. His narrow waist

was crossed by two heavy gun belts, the holsters tied down gunslick fashion.

Nodding curtly to the Mexican, Longarm kept on toward the gate. Suddenly from the tall grass behind him came hoofbeats. He turned in his saddle. Stella Rooney was coming at him, a Winchester across her pommel. He recognized her from the description Sheriff Stallings had given him. She must have been on his tail for some time.

He reined in and waited for her to reach him. When she pulled up alongside him, he noticed at once the graceful curve of her neck and the clean line of her chin. She wore a split buckskin skirt and a leather vest decorated with gleaming conchos over her white blouse. Longarm could not help noticing how her shirt and vest swelled over her full, upthrust breasts. He also could not help noticing her Winchester. Its muzzle was pointing at him.

"All right, mister. Who are you?"

"Point that rifle someplace else and I'll tell you."

She slipped the rifle into her saddle scabbard. "Well?"

"Name's Custis Long." He pulled out his wallet and flashed his badge. "I understand you're the lady who turned Ned Larson in."

"That's right."

"I'd like to ask you a few questions, if I may." Longarm shifted in his saddle. "But not out here."

She gazed coolly at him for a moment longer.

Then she nodded. "I guess that can be arranged."

Spurring ahead of him, she called off the old wrangler and the redhead. The redhead melted back into the bunkhouse and the wrangler returned to the horse barn. Longarm followed her as she rode up to the barn's big entrance, where they both dismounted. The wrangler took the reins of their horses and led them into the barn.

Shaded by a stand of cottonwood, the big house was two stories high with a balcony running along the veranda's roof. Stella Rooney led Longarm across the compound and up the steps onto the veranda. A broadly built Indian housekeeper appeared in the doorway. Stella Rooney addressed her as Blossom and requested some lemonade for her guest and herself. Then she turned to Longarm and indicated with a wave of her hand one of the wicker chairs on the veranda drawn up around a small pine-topped table.

Longarm waited for Stella Rooney to sit first, then sank wearily into the wicker chair. He took off his hat and ran his hand through his mop of tobacco-colored hair. Following his example, Stella Rooney lifted off her straight-brimmed Stetson and unpinned her hair. Then she shook out the thick, chestnut curls, after which she lifted them back off her long graceful neck to let the breeze at it.

"You didn't know I was on your tail, did you?" she said, her eyes flashing.

"No, I didn't. But then I wasn't trying to

27

sneak up on anyone. I figured you'd see me coming—you or one of your hands. By the way, where's the rest of your crew?"

"You've seen them all." She let her hair fall back off her shoulders. "They're not much, I admit. An old beat-up cowpoke and a fresh redhead kid drifted in a few months back."

"You got a habit of taking in strays, looks like."

"It's a bad habit, I admit."

The Indian housekeeper brought out a tray supporting a huge pitcher of lemonade and two tall glasses. Stella Rooney took the tray from her, and leaning close to Longarm, placed it down on the table. Longarm was instantly aware of the indefinable, seductive scent that emanated from her as she filled their glasses. He glanced up at her and saw a single brown curl, damp with moisture, planted against her temple. A single bead of perspiration trailed down her cheek. Her glance met his. He felt a faint stirring in his groin. He thought she blushed in recognition of a mutual attraction, but he could not be sure.

The glasses filled, she sat back down. Longarm took up his and drank deeply, wishing the lemonade was a mite cooler. Stella leaned back in her chair as she drank hers, again lifting her hair to cool her neck.

She smiled at him. "I suppose you would have preferred something stronger."

"This is fine. Thank you, ma'am."

"Well, it's cool and it's wet. That's the best I can do."

"It is more than sufficient, I assure you, ma'am. Now, what can you tell me about Ned Larson."

"That *other* stray I let in."

"Yes."

"You have never met him?"

"I've seen his handiwork."

Her eyes went bleak. "He's a terrible, frightening man, Mr. Long. He does not look at all like what he is. Except perhaps for his eyes. There's a curious, flat deadness in them. At first I found it romantic, trying to imagine what secrets they hid." She shuddered. "Then I found out. I much prefer rattlers. They give warning before they strike and with them you always know what you're dealing with."

"Why did you turn him in?"

"Don't you know?"

"I'd prefer to hear it from you."

"He nearly killed me."

"Why did he turn on you?"

"Because when he admitted to me—actually boasted, in fact—that he was an outlaw, an escaped highwayman, I ordered him off the Lazy J."

"And of course he refused to go."

"Yes. We argued. Then he beat me, so thoroughly, so efficiently, it seemed as if he had taken lessons. He did a near permanent job of it, too. As soon as I recovered I took the buggy

29

into town and told Stallings who he was."

"He let you get away to do that, did he?"

"I took my time about it. I stopped protesting. I let him think I was too terrified of him to turn him in."

"What you did took courage."

"Perhaps. But I see now that I was a fool. I should have blown the bastard away with my Greener."

The easy vehemence with which she uttered this remark startled Longarm. "Are you sure you could have done such a thing?"

She laughed icily. "I assure you, Deputy, I am perfectly capable of doing what has to be done when the time comes."

"What did Larson tell you about himself? Does he have any friends around here?"

"None that I know of, but then Ned never confided in me about anything. About himself and his folks or where he came from, he told me absolutely nothing."

"Do you have any idea where he might have headed?"

"I have a pretty good idea, Deputy."

"Where?"

"Why, right here, to the Lazy J. Ned will be coming back to finish me off. I am certain of it. When I turned him in, he promised he'd escape and come back for me. So far, he's already kept the first part of that promise. I assume he'll be coming by soon enough to keep the second part."

Longarm filled his glass. "As a matter of fact, that's one reason I rode out here. I would have mentioned it sooner, but I didn't want to alarm you."

She laughed shortly and looked away from Longarm, out over the grasslands sloping away beyond the corral. "Ned's a man likes to stalk his prey." She pursed her lips. "I can almost feel him out there right now, making his plans. Getting ready."

Longarm followed her glance and was immediately struck by the fact that the Lazy J's compound was little more than an island in a vast sea of grass. On his ride through this grassland, he had passed heavily larded beef moving through it like fish in an ocean. Hell, the grass was high enough to hide an approaching army, not to mention a single horse and rider.

"You should have more hands," he remarked.

"I will, when it comes branding time. If I last that long. For now, I'll coast. Most of my hands left when I took Ned in. They knew his kind."

"How come you didn't know his kind?"

"You're right, of course. I should have. Maybe I did. But I kept it from myself. With my husband gone, I was . . . a little foolish."

"And human."

She looked at him, her glance bold, unrepentant. "You don't need to make excuses for me, Deputy. And I don't want your sympathy. I knew what I wanted and I took it. I'd do the same thing again if I had the chance. A woman

31

can't wait forever—not out here. And I *am* a woman, Deputy, one who wants the same thing a man does and for the same reason."

He smiled. "I can see that."

"Deputy, what is it that makes a man think that as soon as he drops his pants by a woman's bed, he owns her, lock, stock, and barrel?"

"Maybe it's the same thing that makes a woman marry the first man who says he loves her."

"Yes." She sighed and rested the back of her head against the chair, closing her eyes. "What fools these mortals be. Is that it, Deputy?"

"I reckon so."

"Does that include you, Deputy?"

"Of course."

"And are you possessive?"

"Less than most, I imagine. A man in my line of work doesn't have any right to be possessive. Just grateful."

"You're an interesting man, Deputy."

"My friends call me Longarm."

"You'll stay for the night, of course," she told him. "There's no need for you to sleep in the bunkhouse. There's plenty of room in the house."

"You're very kind."

She smiled. "I hope you'll still think so in the morning."

Ned Larson had been in Lewistown when Longarm returned with Stallings. He had watched

32

from his hotel window as Longarm rode out again, heading southwest—toward the Lazy J, he had no doubt. Good. That made the cheese more binding. He would kill two birds with one stone. When the time came. He had other business right now.

He had seldom visited Lewistown when he had been staying at the Lazy J. He had been perfectly willing to let others pick up what supplies were needed. When he had been hauled out of his jail cell and taken to the station, a few of the townspeople had tried to get a good look at him. But he had not cooperated. He had kept his chin tucked into his chest, his shoulders bowed.

So when he rode into town the night before, no one had paid him the slightest attention. The pimply-faced desk clerk, his face buried in a Ned Buntline dime novel, hardly glanced up as Larson signed the register, snatched up his key and climbed the stairs to his second-floor room.

This morning he had sent the housekeeping maid down for his breakfast and not long ago for his supper. He gave her half a dollar for her trouble. She was so grateful she was anxious to put out for another half-dollar. But he had escorted her from the room. She was fat and had bad teeth. He could not abide crooked teeth in a woman.

It was dark enough now for what he had in mind. Gathering up his gear, he left the room and went down the back stairs. Once in the alley behind the hotel, he followed it to the livery

33

stable. Ducking into it, he hung his gear on a hook beside the chestnut's stall.

The old man who ran the place came sniffing around. He had a pitchfork in his hand.

"It's me, old man," Ned told him. "I'll be ridin' out later tonight. Water my mount and grain him. Not too much, mind."

"Tonight?" The hostler scratched his white head of hair while he tried to get a better look at Ned.

Ned could smell the stench of bad whiskey that came from the hostler like a baleful cloud. "You hard of hearin', old man?" Ned snapped, his voice like cold steel.

"Sure, sure, mister," the hostler said hastily. "Ain't no need to get nasty. I heard you."

"Just make sure the mount's ready."

Ned stepped back out the rear door and slipped down the alley, heading this time for the sheriff's office. He was in no hurry. He had plenty of time. A half hour ago he had seen the sheriff entering the jail house, while his deputy shouldered into the saloon across the street. Ned had come to know the sheriff's and deputy's habits during his stay in the jail house. The sheriff would remain in his office, finishing up his paperwork until his deputy closed the saloon and crossed over to relieve him.

He left the alley that ran alongside the jail house, pushed his hat brim down over his forehead as he passed through a small group of townsmen, kept on to the jail house, and quickly mounted the porch steps. Without a knock he opened the door and stepped inside. Stallings glanced up. Ned smiled and shut the door behind him. His drawn weapon was already cocked. Stallings looked as if a dead man had risen through the floor in front of him.

"Thought you was rid of me, did you, Stallings?"

Stalling's Indian face went hard with resolve. "You're a damn fool comin' back here, Larson. You just put your neck back in the noose."

"And who's goin' to drop it over my neck? You?"

"You can bet I will if I get the chance."

"You talk brave for a dead man."

"I ain't dead yet, you son of a bitch."

Walking over to the side of Stallings's desk, Ned put his right foot against the seat of the sheriff's swivel desk and nudged it quickly back, spilling Stallings out of it. He landed on the floor heavily, his head glancing off the base of the potbellied stove. Dazed, Stallings blinked up at Larson, trying to focus his eyes.

Ned was enjoying himself too much to hurry things. He glanced about for something to use and saw the poker leaning against the wall beside the coal shuttle. He strode over, grabbed it, and returned to the sheriff, who was trying to sit up.

Ned hunkered down and peered closely into

35

Stalling's eyes. He smiled. "How do you feel, you son of a bitch?"

Stallings blinked and tried to shake the cobwebs out.

"Whatsa matter? Cat got your tongue?"

"Bastard . . . !" The sheriff managed at last to struggle to a sitting position.

Ned straightened up, measured carefully, and swung the iron poker.

Flinging up his forearm, Stallings parried the poker, then flung himself at Ned's legs, wrapping both arms around them. Ned lost his balance and fell back against the wall. Propped against it, he managed to bring the poker down across the sheriff's back. With an explosive gasp, the sheriff released Ned's legs. Pulling away, Ned raised the poker and prepared to finish off Stallings when the deputy stepped into the office. Gasping in surprise, he came to a weaving halt. He had apparently drunk his fill at the saloon.

With the speed of a striking cougar, Ned charged the deputy and brought the poker around in a vicious arc. The poker sank into the deputy's neck and nearly tore his head off. Blood splattered the walls. Ned ducked back. His head lolling loosely on his shoulders, the deputy stumbled blindly forward into the office, struck the potbellied stove, then crashed like a tree to the floor.

Glancing at the sheriff, Ned saw that Stallings

had managed to draw his weapon and was hauling it up. Before he could fire, Ned flung the poker down and bolted from the office.

The old hostler was asleep, his back propped against a stall, a bottle of whiskey cradled in his arms. Ned slapped the man's parchment face smartly. The hostler came awake instantly, alarmed. Ned took his bottle and flung it against the wall, shattering it.

The hostler blinked and began to whine. "Hey now, mister! You ain't got no call to do that!"

"Did you water my chestnut?"

"Sure I did."

"And you grained him. Right?"

"I did what you tole me!"

"You rubbed him down too, maybe?"

The old man nodded eagerly.

Ned smiled broadly. "You're a liar!"

Ned stepped back from the old man, his eyes gleaming. He was really seeing someone else. Someone he was recalling from his own past. It happened whenever he came upon any lice-ridden drunk asleep in his piss, cradling a jug. He found himself filled with a sudden, inflaming rage. He kicked the old man in the crotch. Gasping in agony, the hostler twisted about on the stable floor, clutching his genitals.

Ned leaned over him. "You are lucky, old man. I am going to let you live."

The hostler, terrified into sobriety, looked

ready to cry in sheer relief at his deliverance.

"I am not going to kill you because right now I got so much to be thankful for. I am a free man. I got me a fine horse, and once I'm over the border, I'll be joining up with Riel's men. Them Métis are lookin' for men like me—them as know how to handle a gun."

He stepped back from the hostler and peered down at him, the way he would at an insect he had just stomped. The old man was still holding his crotch, but was no longer twisting about on the floor.

Ned dropped two silver coins onto him. They rolled off him and came to rest in a pile of horse manure. "Good-bye, old man. Count your blessings."

A moment later, astride the chestnut, he left the alley and headed for the north end of town. When he reached the wooden plank bridge, he heard distant shouts and glanced back. Shadowy figures were running for the jail house. Smiling, he lifted the chestnut to a canter. When he gained the grassland beyond the town, he kept to the tightly packed grama grass on the ridges so as not to leave any tracks. Gradually, he turned his horse until he was riding due west.

He was heading not for the Canadian border, as he had told the hostler, but for the Lazy J.

Chapter 3

On a grassy knoll behind the cottonwoods Longarm and Stella stood quietly together taking advantage of the cooling breeze. From this spot Longarm could just make out a lone figure riding slowly through the grass, tracing a long circle around the ranch buildings.

This was McWhirter, the young redhead sporting the tied-down holsters. On Longarm's suggestion, he was now circling the ranch and would keep on doing so until dusk. After supper Mac would bed down behind the bunkhouse, not in it, his two six-guns at the ready. Santos, also on Longarm's suggestion, would bed down in the barn loft and keep watch on the ranch house and the grounds surrounding it. At the first sign of Ned Larson's presence, his Sharps would alert the rest of them. This was Longarm's hope, at any rate. He knew he was probably overreacting. Ned Larson might be well on his way to Canada as Billy Vail suggested. Nevertheless, Longarm figured it wouldn't do any harm to take a few precautions.

Shading her eyes, Stella said, "I can barely see Mac."

"He's out there. I just saw him."

"Oh, yes. There he is."

"I told him to keep off the ridges so he wouldn't make himself an easy target."

"A wise precaution."

Longarm watched Mac a moment longer, then glanced at Stella. "He must be a pretty strong kid. I mean, to be able to carry around all that heavy artillery..."

Stella laughed softly. "Poor Mac. He is such a kid. Santos says he is always reading those dime novels about the West. I saw him out back once practicing his fast draw."

"How was he doing?"

She laughed softly, almost fondly. "He dropped his guns more than once and never came near hitting the tin cans he'd placed on a tree stump."

"I wish I hadn't asked," Longarm commented, "but I suspected as much." His eyes caught Mac's dim figure a moment before he vanished into a swale. "But he'll learn. He'll damn well have to."

"I hope it isn't Ned who teaches him," Stella said. "It's liable to be his last lesson."

Longarm sensed Stella's uneasiness. "Ned would be a fool to come back here," he tried to assure her. "His best bet would be to head north for the border."

"That's what a normal man *would* do, Long-arm. But Ned is not a normal man."

"I guess you're right."

"I am, Longarm. Believe me."

"I believe you, Stella."

Longarm saw her trembling slightly, even though the breeze had dropped off completely. It was the memory of Ned Larson that chilled her. He sat down crosslegged. Stella reclined length-wise in the tall grass beside him. She rested on her elbows and looked at him.

"You said there was a deadness in Ned Lar-son's eyes. You got any idea what makes this bastard tick, Stella?"

She plucked a long grass stem and began suck-ing on it. "Yes. A deep bitterness, an all-consum-ing hatred," she replied carefully. "I caught glimpses of it occasionally, and it wasn't pleasant. He is a fine-looking young man and at times has a wonderful grin. He can be fun to be around. But when the mood is on him, the sun vanishes behind a cloud and he becomes someone else. Someone cold. Ruthless. Without any feelings at all. In the end I realized that he felt no warmth for anybody, including himself. Empty would be a good word to describe him. Yes. That's it. He's empty inside. A hollow man."

"Not a pleasant picture. But I've seen his like before. Usually they are cold-blooded killers."

"That's Ned Larson. A killer. He has no mercy. No compunction. He'll do whatever it takes to get his way. And there's something else

41

. . . I don't think he cares very much if he lives or dies."

"That makes him quite a package."

"Just think of the people he has killed already."

Yes. This grisly fact had once again crossed Longarm's mind. What made finding this vicious killer doubly difficult was the fact that they had no idea where Ned Larson had come from before surfacing during that botched robbery. Like so many others who put the more civilized East behind them, he found the West an ideal hunting ground.

Dusk was falling rapidly now. Even from this distance, Longarm thought he could smell the meal Blossom was preparing for them. He pushed himself upright, turned, and took Stella's hand to pull her to her feet. When he did so, she rose upright easily, allowing herself to halt within inches of him, the thrust of her breasts warm against Longarm's shirt front. The sweet smell of her was a heady perfume. He thought he would like to kiss her and that she would like him to kiss her. But they had only just met that day, and the grim subject of their conversation seemed to hang in the air between them.

Maybe later. This night perhaps.

As if she were thinking the same thing, she brushed close by him, her hand still clasped firmly in his, and led him off the knoll back down toward the cottonwoods.

• • •

The lock on the bedroom door clicked. Awake instantly, Longarm sat up, his hand already closing about the grips of his .44. The door swung open. Stella stood naked in the doorway, a pale alabaster statue in the moonlight. Longarm released the Colt and sat up. She stepped into the room and closed the door behind her, then strode boldly across the room toward him, her dark pubic triangle gleaming in the moonlight.

"I had hoped to surprise you asleep."

"I'm a light sleeper."

"I'm glad you don't object."

"Now, why in hell would I do that?"

She was close enough for him to smell the hot closeness of her. The dark, shimmering waves of her thick hair reached clear down to her upthrust nipples. He reached out and placed his hands on her flaring hips, then drew her down beside him. He was naked under the fresh sheets and she was under him in an instant, her thighs yawning wide for him. He shifted so he could look down at her and drank in the sight of her rounded curves, full breasts, the swell of her belly, the dark gleaming night of her pubis.

She stirred impatiently under him. "Please," she muttered huskily. "I'm ready for you. Now!"

He chuckled and bent his head to take her bullet-hard nipples between his lips, his tongue flicking them wickedly. With a deep sigh, she lunged herself up at him and flung her arms about his neck, drawing him down hungrily onto her.

"You are a devil!" she whispered huskily into his ear.

Longarm kissed her on the lips, then sank deep into her, cleaving her soft warmth until he was deep within her, their two bodies completely merged. Stella gasped delightedly. He drove still deeper with a sudden lunge that set her shuddering, her breath coming now in short, ragged gasps.

"Stay inside me," she directed him. "Don't move. Just press in deeper."

He leaned into her.

"Deeper," she groaned.

Longarm did his best and felt her shudder under him. "Now," she whispered. "Do me now! Make me come, lover!"

He pounded into her then, riding her like the wild bronco she suddenly became, bearing down savagely with each thrust, grunting, his knees digging into the bed, aware of himself building to his climax—then surging over the top, gasping wildly. Abruptly the breath rushed from her throat in one long, expiring moan. Crying out, she shuddered, then began exploding beneath him like a string of firecrackers.

After a long, delicious moment, it was over. She blew her cheeks out, beads of perspiration standing out on her forehead, her cheeks glowing.

Looking down at her, Longarm smiled. "How was that?"

"Lovely, just lovely. But we're not through

yet," she insisted. "I can feel you inside me. You're still big enough!"

"Maybe it's stuck."

"Fool! Drive in deeper! Deeper. I want every inch of you!"

Longarm complied. Bracing his knees, he lunged forward and kept thrusting, feeling himself growing within her. She gasped as she built rapidly to another climax. He felt the muscles of her stomach contracting convulsively under his muscular belly.

"This time," she gasped, "come when I do."

"Is that important?"

"Do it!"

He was already way ahead of her and in no mood to hold back as he surged on, driving into her with two more violent thrusts. A second later he was shuddering violently, draining himself completely this time in a long, sustained spasm that matched her own. When it was complete, he held himself pressed hard against her soft body, pulsing savagely, mindlessly until at last he was emptied. A sigh of contentment came from deep within her and he rolled off her.

She stretched out her long legs and turned to look at him, her dark eyes smoky with satiety. Longarm leaned closer and kissed her gently on her glowing cheeks. She held him to her for a moment, murmuring softly.

"That was lovely," she told him, falling back and staring up at the ceiling. "Perhaps Ned Larson will not come back here and you can wait for him for a long, long time."

"I admit, the prospect is a pleasant one. But I want Ned. If he doesn't return here, I am going to have to go after him."

"Well, no need to be in a hurry," she told him softly. "Stay here."

"Sure. For now."

"Mmmm," she said. "You are so agreeable."

He lay flat on his back and looked up at the ceiling. Why not be agreeable? Staying here would be no chore. It was still his best course of action. Ned was a killer. Longarm knew the type. To even a score such men usually lost sight of reality.

"Oh, my," Stella said softly. "Look at that."

Longarm looked down at his crotch. It amazed even him.

"You are some kind of man," she whispered delightedly, reaching down with her long fingers and closing them about his renewed shaft.

"It was all that riding," Longarm explained lamely. "Worked me up, it must've."

"My dear," Stella said, stroking him gently, "there is no need for you to apologize."

She swung her thigh over his pelvis and crouched above him, her dark hair falling over him like a tent. She bent and let her full, incandescent breasts sweep over his chest. Then she kissed him, laughing mischievously. His erection was growing like an eager plant in the sunlight, thrusting impudently up between her legs.

She chuckled and leaned back. Her hand knifed down to guide him into her. Then she sat back. He felt himself thrusting up deep into her and heard her sigh as she took all of him. Her muscle control was astounding. It felt as if her fist was closing about his throbbing shaft.

He gasped.

"Now it is my turn to pleasure you," she told him eagerly.

She began to rock gently. He reached up for her breasts. Once again her nipples sprang to life under his rough caress. Then his hands explored further, reveling in the silken smooth warmth of her shimmering body. She began to rise and fall now with greater urgency, grunting like a cougar, leaning as far forward over him as she did so he could take her breasts in his mouth. She cried out in delight when he did, flicking at them with his tongue until her nipples became rigid. By this time she was slamming down upon his erection with an abandon that aroused him to a fiery urgency of his own. He grabbed her flaring hips and slammed her repeatedly, furiously down onto his shaft. In a moment he exploded.

She felt it, gurgled deeply, and came herself, clinging to him. He felt her hot juices streaming down his long shaft. "Yes! Yes! Yes!..." she cried softly.

She collapsed forward onto his chest. He ran his hands through her hair and held her close. For a long moment they said nothing. At last she rolled off him and propped herself onto her elbow and smiled dreamily at him.

"Mmmm," she murmured softly. "That was lovely."

She kissed him lightly, playfully, on his nose, then left the bed and walked regally to the door, her pale figure glowing in the moonlight, her heavy tresses flaring out behind her like a dark cape. In a moment she had vanished, the door clicking lightly behind her.

Longarm reached in under his pillow and closed his right hand about the grips of his .44 and tumbled headlong into an exhausted sleep.

Ned Larson hobbled his big chestnut beside a creek half a mile from the Lazy J. He glanced appreciatively up at the bright moon, then started off through the waist-high grass. In less than an hour he crested a rise and saw the cottonwoods in the distance. A dark patch against the night sky. The outline of the big house barely visible. He rested his Winchester on his shoulder and came to a halt. The ranch buildings were dark. The only light came from the bright moon overhead. He started up again. A spooked steer lurched upright in the grass in front of him, swayed uncertainly, then charged swiftly off through the grass.

Ned kept on. The rear of the big horse barn loomed out of the night. He came to the corral, climbed over it silently, then ran lightly across it to the rear of the barn. Nudging open the back door, he slipped into its pitch-black interior and slammed headfirst into a pitchfork handle. Cursing, he flung the pitchfork aside and plunged on toward the ladder in the far corner leading to the loft. Running into the pitchfork's handle had caused a surge of unreasonable anger. Still fuming, he reached the ladder and climbed swiftly to the loft, making no effort to move quietly. Swaying upright in the loft's dim interior, he noticed that the hay-loading door was open. Something or someone was sprawled on the floor behind it. Crouching low, he moved closer and saw it was an empty sleeping bag. Before he could straighten up to look around, a rifle barrel struck him in the small of the back.

Dropping his rifle, he staggered forward. His foot caught on a roof strut and he sprawled forward onto a pile of hay. Flinging himself over onto his back, he drew his Colt. Santos stepped closer and kicked the weapon out of his hand.

Hell's fire! What was *he* doing up here?

Santos raised his Sharps. Ned flung himself at the old man, struck him high on the chest and twisted the rifle out of his grasp. Santos staggered back. Following after him, Ned swung the Sharp's barrel and caught the man in the side. Santos gasped and folded over.

"You expected me," Ned told Santos as he writhed on the floor. "You were waiting up here for me to show."

The old man's white head nodded faintly.

Ned went down on one knee beside him.

"What's that old man? I couldn't hear you."

"*Sí! Sí!,*" the old man gasped. "*Sí!* I wait up here for you."

"Who put you up to it? Stella?"

"No."

"Who, then?"

"It was my idea. I tell Miss Stella you will come back. And she believe me. So I come up here to wait for you."

Ned frowned. He didn't believe Santos. The old man was too tough to spill his guts this easily, no matter how ill he was used. He was holding his side, his head turned about so he could look up at Ned. His liquid eyes burned with a fierce loathing.

"I don't believe you, old man. You don't have that much sense."

Santos said nothing.

"Where's the kid?"

"I don't know."

Ned slapped the old man in the face. In the quiet loft it sounded like a pistol shot. "Old man, tell me where Mac is or I'll finish you right now."

"I don't know, pig!"

Ned considered his next move. He could not shoot the old man. He wanted no sound to alert the kid and Stella to his presence. He had the drop on them now and he wanted to keep it. He would have to kill Santos as silently as he could. He stood up. Santos cowered on the loft floor beneath him. Holding Santos's Sharps by the barrel, Ned lifted the stock over his shoulder and brought it down swiftly, aiming for the old man's head.

But Santos sprang to life. With astonishing alacrity, he rolled away from the descending barrel and leaped to his feet. Darting for the open loft door, he plunged through it and dropped to the ground below. Ned ran over to the loft door and saw Santos's dim figure limping across the yard toward the big house. No longer concerned with silence, Ned tracked Santos as he struggled up the veranda steps and pulled the Sharps's trigger. The round ricocheted off a veranda post. Santos pushed open the door and vanished inside.

Ned flung the Sharps to the loft floor. Let it be, then. Stella and the old Mexican were inside, and Ned was outside. This was a game he could play. He turned back around and poked through the hay for his Colt. He found it, then picked up his Winchester and clambered back down the ladder. He had a pretty good idea where the kid was. In the bunkhouse or behind it. If Ned remembered correctly, the kid was all bluff with shit for a backbone. Ned would go find him. Talk to him maybe. Or kill him. It all depended.

Then he would settle down for the siege.

The crack of the Sharps brought Longarm bolt upright, his Colt swinging out in front of him. A moment later came the sound of someone entering the house. The bedroom door burst open. It was Stella.

"Someone's inside!" she told him, her voice hushed.

"I heard."

Longarm burst past her and out into the hallway, as naked as a plucked chicken and just as vulnerable. Halfway down the hallway, he pulled up. A shadow loomed suddenly before him. Then he saw Santos's white head and heard the man groaning. As he started up again, Santos collapsed to the floor.

Keeping pace with Longarm, Stella cried, "Santos! What is it?"

"That devil. Ned! He ees back!"

"You shot?" Longarm asked, bending over him.

"No! It is my ankle. I hurt it some when I jump from loft."

"Where's Ned?"

"Outside! In the barn, I think!"

"Stay here with Santos," Longarm told Stella. "I'm going after him!"

Longarm ducked back to his bedroom, pulled on his pants, stomped into his boots, and snatching up his Winchester, left the house. He emerged onto the front veranda and crouched low, crabbing sideways the moment the door closed behind him. He thought then of the kid behind the bunkhouse and dropped off the veranda. Keeping to the shadows, he ran to the bunkhouse and ducked behind it.

"Hey, Mac!" he whispered hoarsely. "You back here?"

There was no response. The kid was not there. So where the hell was he?

Keeping low, Ned had been a few feet from the horse trough when he saw the big fellow burst out of the house. He froze and ducked behind the trough. Who the hell was this? And then he remembered the U.S. deputy marshal he'd seen riding out of town. The bastard had got here then, just as he'd figured. Two birds with one stone, sure enough. Ned watched the big man crab sideways, then drop off the porch and disappear in the direction of the bunkhouse.

That left a clear path to the house. And Stella. He left the cover of the horse trough and headed toward the veranda. The kid stepped out from behind the corner of the bunkhouse.

"Hold it right there, Ned!" he called. His voice quavered nervously.

"How you doin', Mac?" Ned called. "Long time no see."

"Never mind that," the kid croaked. "Drop that rifle."

"You don't need to take that tone with me, kid. No reason why we got to get in a tangle. I got no cause to go against you." Ned smiled. "Maybe we could ride out of here together when I finish this here business."

The kid took a step away from the bunkhouse and raised his rifle to his shoulder. "You ain't finishin' no business," the kid said. "Not here, you ain't."

Ned ducked low and flung himself back behind the water trough. The kid's rifle cracked. The round exploded harmlessly in the ground in front of the trough. Ned propped his rifle on the lip of the trough, aimed at the kid, and squeezed off a shot. The slug took out a piece of siding near the kid's head. Ned fired again. The kid appeared to buckle. He vanished from sight.

The big fellow had come around the bunkhouse by this time and took the kid's place. He raised his rifle and began pouring a steady fire into the trough. Ned ducked low as the rounds slammed into the wooden trough, a few whining off the pump handle. Ned flung himself flat, tucked his own Winchester's stock into his shoulder and, levering swiftly, sent a withering fire back at the big man, forcing him to duck out of sight behind the bunkhouse.

Leaving his rifle behind, Ned drew his Colt, scrambled to his feet, and broke for the big house. Not a single shot chased him as he clambered up the veranda steps and burst inside.

Stella had ordered Blossom to stay in her room next to the pantry while she stationed herself at the front window beside Santos. She held in her right hand a Smith & Wesson revolver. The room was dark so she could follow the action outside in the yard.

When she glimpsed Ned's form racing for the

house, she left Santos and ran to the living room doorway. As Ned burst through the door and into the entry, she fired point blank at him. Incredibly, she missed. Ned was on her with the speed of a striking rattler. He grabbed her wrist and twisted cruelly. Crying out, she dropped her revolver. Limping grotesquely, Santos pushed through the living room doorway behind her and lunged for Ned. Ned chopped down viciously with the barrel of his six-gun and caught Santos on the back of his head. The old man sagged to the floor.

Ned grabbed Stella and pulled her close. "Thought you'd never see me again, didn't you!"

Stella slapped him so sharply, her palm stung. Ned pulled back, his grin gone, then kicked her in the stomach. She knifed to the hallway floor, clutching at her midsection, gasping for breath. Ned kicked her again, this time in the face. Stella felt the numbing shock of his boot, then little more as she slipped into semiconsciousness. Only dimly was she aware of Ned dragging her down the hallway.

In the kitchen he propped her up in a chair and leaned his face close to hers. "I think I just learned you something, ain't that right?"

Stella was in no condition to reply.

He grinned. "You don't have to talk if you can't. Just nod your head."

But she could not nod her head or shake it. The kitchen whirled about her head sickeningly. She was panting with the awful pain that had exploded in her stomach. Her head felt as if it were growing rapidly larger. All she could manage was an obscenity, one only men were supposed to use.

This amused him. "A woman who can talk like that gets me interested, sure enough."

He went to the kitchen window and glanced out. Then he turned to look her over, his eyes cruel. Clutching the tabletop, she hauled herself upright.

"I think maybe I'll take you with me, Stella. You can keep me company during the long nights. Don't think you can escape. I got friends in them mountains. There'll be a cabin and plenty of grub, especially when I bring them gents a real professional whore to amuse them. Hell, you'll only be doing what comes natural."

She flung a pitcher full of sugar at him. Laughing, he ducked easily. Shattering the window, the sugar bowl disappeared through it.

"Temper! Temper!" Ned said, striding over to her.

She ducked away and felt the barrel of his six-gun slam against the side of her head. She staggered back against the wall, then slid down it to the floor.

"Shit!" Ned cried.

She looked up. Blossom was standing in her open doorway, a huge butcher knife gleaming in her hand. With stolid ferocity, she lunged across the kitchen and began slicing down at Ned. As he warded off her plunging blade, he managed to thrust the muzzle of his revolver into her ample midsection and squeeze the trigger. Blossom's heavy body muffled the detonation. The big woman trembled and settled to the floor, the knife falling from her hand.

Wild with fury, Stella scrambled to her feet, picked up a chair and brought it down on Ned's head and shoulders, shattering it. Uttering a confused grunt, Ned staggered back and pushed himself dazedly out through the kitchen door. Stella heard him stumble and fall. Snatching up the butcher knife, she went to the open door. On his feet now, Ned turned and flung a wild shot at her. The night swallowed him up.

She slammed the door shut, then hurried over to Blossom's prostrate form. The woman's eyes were closed and she was breathing fitfully. A dark flow of blood poured out of the wound in her belly.

Stella began to cry.

Longarm had already sent the kid in through the front door. Rounding the house, he was in time to see Ned Larson stumble out, fling a shot back at Stella in the open doorway, then vanish into the cottonwoods. Cursing in frustration, Longarm followed after him.

The son of a bitch was like a murderous will-o'-the-wisp, as elusive as a barnyard fly. Deep in the cottonwoods, Longarm held up to listen for the sound of Larson's flight through the brush. When he heard it, faintly, off to his right, he followed. There was no reason for Larson to know anyone was tracking him, so Longarm kept after him as silently as a shadow, pausing every now and then to listen.

When he no longer heard Ned moving ahead of him through the night, he pulled up and took a deep breath, peering about him bleakly, searching for any movement in the shadowy stand of cottonwoods. The blackness of the night was lit only dimly by a high, silver-plated moon.

He was thinking of turning back toward the house when he heard a sound on his right. He spun. Ned Larson was coming at him from less than ten feet away. The revolver in his hand detonated. Longarm felt a powerful impact in his left shoulder. Reeling backward, he struck a tree and toppled to the ground beside it. Larson fired repeatedly down at him, his face demonic in the light from his gun flashes. But it was dark and Ned was too crazed to take the time to aim carefully. The first slug pounded into the ground beside Longarm. The second bit into the tree trunk inches from his head.

Longarm was still holding his Colt. Without conscious volition, he fired up at Larson. The man ducked back, sent one more futile shot down at Longarm, then bolted back into the trees. Longarm took a deep breath, pushed himself wearily to his feet, and headed back toward the house.

Before he reached it, the numbness in his shoulder faded, and a steady, gnawing pain took its place. He treated it with the contempt it deserved. By rights, he should have been a dead man by now.

So why lose any sleep over a slug in his shoulder?

Chapter 4

Like survivors from a disaster, the four were gathered in the living room, the only light coming from the moonlight streaming in through the open windows. Santos crouched at one window, Mac at another. Beside Longarm on the couch, Stella was winding a bandage tightly over his shoulder wound. She had already cleaned it with a generous mix of whiskey and water. The slug had gone completely through his shoulder, carrying with it a chunk of flesh and muscle. Fortunately, the slug had missed his shoulder bone, and despite some discomfort, he was still able to use his left arm.

Santos had a painfully swollen ankle as a result of his leap from the barn loft. With a bedroom sheet torn into strips, Stella had bound the ankle tightly, enabling him to hobble about. In his exchange with Ned Larson, Mac had sustained a flesh wound on his right thigh. He had taken care of it himself and insisted on ignoring it. That he had not been able to stop Ned when he had the man in his sights first bewildered, then angered him. Now he peered out eagerly into the night, hoping for a glimpse of his quarry —for not one of them denied that Larson was out there somewhere in the dark night. Prowling. Watching the house. Getting ready to raise hell itself.

"There, how's that?" Stella asked as she finished snugging the bandage about Longarm's shoulder.

"Fine," Longarm told her, flexing his left arm. "It's stiff, but I can use the arm."

Stella glanced nervously toward the windows, then leaned back and blew a lock of hair off her forehead. She had recovered somewhat from the death of Blossom, but it had been a shattering blow to her. Her eyes were still puffy from crying. Longarm had dragged the big woman from the kitchen, and she was laid out now on her bed, growing cold. Until daylight, there was nothing more anyone could do.

"You say Ned planned to kidnap you," Longarm said to Stella.

"Not exactly. He wasn't thinking of ransom."

"Where did he want to take you?"

"The mountains. Said something about a cabin. And having friends there." She shuddered. "It seems he is anxious to share me with them."

"A cabin. Not a town."

"No. Not a town."

"That means a hole in the wall somewhere, a box canyon maybe, where outlaws could hunker down for the winter. It will sure as hell be well guarded."

"I should think so. Wherever it is, I'm certainly glad he's not going to be able to take me there."

"Thanks to Blossom."

"Hey!" cried Mac from the window. "Look at that!"

Longarm and Stella hurried over to the open window and peered out. A shadowy figure was fleetingly visible leading two horses from the barn. It was Ned Larson, obviously. With each hand on a bridle, Larson kept himself between the animals as he led them into the corral behind the barn. A moment later he led two more horses out. Santos tried to track him with his Sharps, but he could barely see the man, and he did not want to chance hitting one of the horses.

"What the hell's he up to?" Mac asked.

"Well, it's a lead pipe cinch he didn't come back here to steal four horses."

A moment later they noticed a glow in the barn's rear. One of the floor-level windows winked redly.

"Son of a bitch!" Stella muttered furiously.

"Ess set barn on fire!" Santos muttered.

A sudden, leaping brightness filled the night, bringing a garish daylight to the compound. Longarm shook his head in frustration as he watched the flames leap almost immediately into the barn's loft. A moment later the flames ate through the front wall, and before long broke out onto the roof, sending black plumes of smoke pumping high enough to blot out the moon.

"Dammit," muttered Mac, his rifle up to his chin like Santos, "I don't see no sign of the bastard."

Muttering an oath, Longarm stepped away from the window. "Stay here, Santos," he told the Mexican. Then he turned to Mac. "Let's go, Mac. Time we got that bastard."

While they were transfixed at the sight of that burning barn, Longarm had suddenly realized Ned Larson could have been coming at them from the rear. He plunged through the kitchen and slammed out the back door, Mac on his heels.

The light from the blazing barn sent a lurid glow even this far into the cottonwoods. "Circle around that way," Longarm told Mac, indicating his left. "I'll go this way."

Mac nodded and disappeared into the cottonwoods. Longarm cut around the side of the house, then glanced back. He thought he saw a figure ducking into the trees. Ignoring the ache in his shoulder, he cut after the shadowy figure. About fifty yards into the cottonwoods, at the edge of a small clearing, he pulled up to get his bearings. His earlier loss of blood was telling on him. His head spun slightly. He reached out and grabbed a tree trunk to steady himself. Across the clearing Mac stepped into view.

"Watch out, Longarm!" he cried.

A rifle cracked on Longarm's right. Mac

crumpled to the ground. Longarm swung his rifle and fired twice at Ned Larson's blurred figure ducking back into the trees. Hoping for a clear shot, Longarm took off after him. But he realized soon enough he was chasing smoke. He pulled up and hurried back through the darkness to where he had seen Mac go down. Mac was propped up against a tree waiting for him. In an effort to staunch the blood flowing from his wound, he was holding his hand tightly against the hole in his side.

"The bullet still in there?" Longarm asked.

"Nope. But it ripped me bad."

"You shouldn't't've stepped into view like that."

"Ned had you in his sights. I could see him. You couldn't."

Longarm pulled away Mac's shirt and examined his wound. The bullet had entered just above his hipbone. The exit wound was a big one, from which blood issued in a steady dark stream. Already Longarm could see a marked paleness on Mac's face.

Leaning his rifle against a tree, Longarm picked Mac up and carried him back through the trees to the house, uncomfortably aware that he and Mac had let themselves be lured deep into the cottonwoods a considerable distance from the house. He did not like it when he saw the back door wide open. Inside, Santos was lying facedown in the middle of the floor.

There was no sign of Stella.

Longarm let Mack down on the sofa and hurried over to Santos. The old man had a bloody gash in his forehead. Longarm shook him until the Mexican's eyes flickered, then opened.

"Where's Stella?"

"Larson...he take her. I could not stop him."

In obvious pain Santos leaned his head back down on the carpet and closed his eyes. Longarm stood up. The sudden clatter of hooves sounded. Moving swiftly to the window, he saw Ned Larson and Stella flash past the still-burning barn and vanish into the night. In that brief glimpse, Longarm saw Stella's hands tied securely to the saddle horn.

Ned was heading west for that hidden canyon deep in the mountains he had told her about—and he was taking Stella with him.

As Longarm rode into Lewistown late the next day, Sheriff Stallings strode out onto the small porch in front of his office and nodded a greeting to Longarm and his two wounded sidekicks. Santos had wound a crude bandage around his forehead, and the kid—tight-lipped and pale—rode slumped painfully over his saddle horn. Longarm himself rode with his left hand tucked into his frock coat to rest his injured shoulder. Undoubtedly, the three of them presented a dismal, unlucky spectacle to the sheriff and the rest of the townsmen who were already streaming down the street toward them.

Longarm nudged his horse into the hitch rail in front of the jail house and dismounted. "Send for a doc, will you, Sheriff. The kid here's been shot."

Stallings caught sight of a clerk with a green eyeshade hurrying up. "Clem! Get hold of Doc Holt!"

The clerk turned quickly and bolted back through the growing crowd. Longarm eased the kid out of his saddle, then helped Santos dismount. The three climbed the steps wearily and entered the sheriff's office. Santos limped painfully over to a wooden chair under the gun rack. Mac went straight to the cot along the wall and flopped wearily down upon it, his eyes closing almost immediately. It had not been an easy ride. He was done in completely.

"Where's Stella Rooney?" Stallings asked Longarm.

Longarm slacked into the chair by Stallings's desk and shucked his hat back off his forehead. "Gone."

"Gone? Gone where?"

"Ned Larson's taken her."

Stallings swore and slumped into his own seat. "My God, Longarm. What happened?"

Longarm told him.

Stallings looked pained as he absorbed this development, then gave a vivid and depressing account of Larson's last night in town. When he finished his grisly account of Larson's attack on him and on his deputy, now resting six feet underground, Longarm found himself amazed at Larson's limitless capacity for murderous behavior.

At that moment the clerk entered with the doctor. With only a cursory glance at Longarm, he hurried over to McWhirter, examined the kid's wound, then went back out onto the porch and beckoned two men from the crowd into the office and told them to escort the kid to his office. As the kid left, the doc checked Santos's head and ankle, then Longarm's shoulder wound, after which he pronounced both men fit. He hurried from the sheriff's office then to see to Mac.

Longarm looked at the sheriff. "I need a drink."

"I could use one, too."

With Santos limping beside them, the two men made their way through the thinning crowd in front of the sheriff's office, entered the saloon across the street and found a quiet table in a corner. A few townsmen, eager for news, pushed into the saloon after them, but respected the trio's obvious desire for privacy.

Longarm had noted a grimace on the sheriff's face as he eased himself into his chair, and remembered that the man had fought off a poker-wielding Ned Larson. "How do you feel, Stallings? From what you tell me, Larson didn't exactly treat you gently."

"I'm all right. Just beat up and sore. I'm more purple than white for now."

The barkeep brought over their beer.

"Anyway," continued the sheriff, "it's clear what Ned told the hostler was designed to throw us off his trail. It sure as hell wasn't Canada he was heading for, it was the Lazy J. Trouble is, the ruse worked, or I would've headed out for the Lazy J to warn you."

"Right now, if I can believe what he told Stella, he's headin' west. For the mountains."

"Makes sense. Since I got back here, I been askin' around. There's a hole-in-the-wall gang in there somewhere, from what I been hearin'. A canyon, maybe. But you can be pretty damn sure it'll be well guarded."

"You got any idea how I could find this canyon? Any special landmarks?"

The sheriff shook his head. "You might as well be looking for a needle in a haystack. A lot of men have gone in there, but there ain't many have come back out. That's wild, rugged country, and most of it is pointed straight up."

Longarm shrugged wearily. "Then I'll just have to track the bastard."

"That won't be easy."

"I know that."

The three men drank their beer in silence for a while, lost in their own gloomy thoughts.

It was Stallings who spoke up first. "When'll you be headin' out, Longarm?"

"Soon as I can. Right now I got a bum left shoulder. I can't handle a rifle worth a damn.

Too shaky. And I want to be sure the kid's all right before I light out."

"You mean you've takin' a liking to that two-gun redhead, have you?"

"The kid saved my life back there. The slug he took was the price he paid for warning me. What about you, Stallings? You want to come along?"

Stallings shook his head. "I'd like to, Longarm. Nothing I'd like better than to help you finish off that rattlesnake. The trouble is you got to bring him in alive. If I got him in my sights, I would let no man stop me from pulling the trigger." He sighed and lifted the beer to his lips. "Besides, them mountains are way the hell out of my jurisdiction."

Santos spoke up quickly. "I will ride with you, *Señor* Long."

"You don't need to, Santos," Longarm told him.

"Why you say that? You think I am too old?"

"Hell, no."

"Bueno," the old man said, brightening. "I am not too old. And I have score to settle with that devil."

Devil, Longarm thought. Yes. That was as good a tag as any for Ned Larson.

Larson and Stella reached the settler's place well after midnight. The cabin was dark, its occupants no doubt asleep. The night air was clammy and cold. Stella shivered and tried to keep her teeth from chattering. They had ridden on past dusk without pause, Ned using as guide the tracery of wood smoke he had last glimpsed on the horizon.

He dismounted behind the settler's horse barn, then pulled Stella off her horse and proceeded to bind her securely to a fence post.

"Why are we stopping here?" Stella asked.

"We need grub, provisions."

He looked into her eyes. Even in the stars' dim light he could see her bright eagerness to cross him. He saw the fear, too.

"Are you going to pay for what you take?" she asked bitterly. "Or just take what you want —the way you take everything else?"

"Now why would these shit-kickers want cash? They'll be eager to help us two pilgrims. They're gonna be glad to contribute."

"I see," she said bitterly. "You're going to rob them."

"What do you care?"

"All right, then. Go on in there. I don't care."

He laughed softly. She wasn't foolin' him none. Soon as he got to the cabin, she'd open her mouth and yell her fool head off to warn the sodbuster. He untied his bandanna and balled it up and thrust it into her mouth, then wrapped rawhide around her mouth. She struggled as he worked and tried to kick him. Grinning, he danced back, waited a moment, then slapped her hard on the side of the head to see if the gag held. It held. She slumped back against the post and glared at him with blazing eyes.

He left her and unstrapped the saddlebags. Draping them over his shoulders, he snaked his rifle out of its scabbard, circled the barn and approached the house. He moved carefully, on the alert for a dog. He had already decided that if one came for him, he would shoot it and burst into the house and silence its occupants as quickly as possible.

There was no dog. Instead, he almost stepped on a Rhode Island red nesting close by the low front porch. As he drew quickly back, the hen squawked indignantly and fluttered away, clucking loudly. Ned froze. But no sound came from the cabin and no lantern glowed suddenly in its interior. He stepped up onto the low, weathered front porch. The boards gave under him. But in the damp night, there was no telltale creak. He reached for the door. There was no lock on it. It hung loosely on worn leather hinges.

Pushing it open, he stepped inside. From the smell of baked bread that hung in the air, he knew at once he was in the kitchen. Two closed doors led off it. A bedroom and a living room, more than likely. He walked over to the deal table in the middle of the kitchen, took off the lamp's chimney, scratched a match and lit the wick, turned it up full, and replaced the chimney. Then he placed his rifle and saddlebags down on the table, pulled out a chair, and sat down facing the two doors.

He had made no effort to be quiet when he strode across the room and pulled out the chair. he sat in it now, waiting, took out his makings and built himself a smoke. Raising the lamp's chimney, he leaned forward and lit the cigarette. Sitting back, he inhaled deeply. The keen sense of excitement he had felt on entering the cabin was fading. He became impatient. He did not plan to sit here all night.

He cleared his throat loudly, then scraped the chair back a few inches, the harsh sound filling the dark kitchen. He took a long drag on his cigarette. As he exhaled, the bedroom door opened. A gaunt, bearded man in long johns stepped cautiously into the kitchen, blinking in the sudden light. Ned regarded him with measured contempt. The man's long johns were filthy. His lined face was grimy. His long nails were caked with black soil.

"Who the hell're you, mister?" the sodbuster asked. Behind him, his wife's pale face peered out at Ned with wide, frightened eyes.

Ned straightened in his chair and lifted his rifle off the table. "Just a pilgrim passin' through, friend."

The sodbuster swallowed unhappily, and with his right hand pushed his wife back into the bedroom.

Ned stood up, smiling coldly. "What's the matter?" he asked. "Don't you want me to meet your lovely wife?"

"No, I don't."

"That's not very friendly."

"I don't care what it is," the nester said heatedly. "You damn well get out of here!" His voice quavered with a mixture of anger and fear.

Ned levered a fresh cartridge into his rifle's firing chamber and got to his feet. "No need to get your bowels in an uproar, nester. Like I said, I'm a pilgrim passing through, and I happen to need some provisions."

A hopeful gleam sprang into the nester's eyes. He moistened his lips. "All right. Take what you need. Then get out."

Ned casually laid his rifle down on the table, turned his back on the nester, and walked over to the cupboards. He opened one of the cabinets and reached up for a can of beans. He heard the nester lunge toward him. Pulling his six-gun, Ned whirled. The muzzle of his revolver was only inches from the nester's chest when he fired. The slug punched a neat hole in his dirty nightshirt and exploded out of his back, spraying blood over the chair Ned had just left. With the barrel of his six-gun, Ned slammed the dazed man on the head and drove him to his knees. As he collapsed facedown onto the floor, Ned heard the nester's wife sob and cry out. Ned glanced at the bedroom door as the woman slammed it shut. He heard her pushing something heavy against it.

Ned stepped to the door and put his shoulders against it and shoved. He heard the dresser—if that was what it was—sliding back over the wooden floor. Barely inches from his head came the sound of the woman's hard breathing as she lent her own weight to that of the dresser. Smiling, Ned kept pushing. He enjoyed the contest. The door gradually opened wider until there was enough room for him to slip through into the bedroom. The nester's wife lunged at him, her bony fists pounding futilely about his head and shoulders. He pushed her back. She stumbled. He raised his Colt. In the dimness of the room, he could not see her clearly, but shot anyway. He heard her gasp and saw her slump to the floor. Walking close to get a better view of her, he fired twice more into her crumpled form.

As the terrific detonations faded in the small room, he became aware of the wailing screech of an infant coming from a small crib in the corner. He walked over, picked up the babe, crib and all, and took it outside the cabin. Placing the crib down in the yard some distance from the cabin, he rocked it until the babe quieted and dropped back into sleep. Ned looked down at the sleeping infant for a moment or two, then returned to the kitchen and filled the saddlebags with provisions. Slinging the loaded saddlebags over his shoulders, he picked up the lamp and hurled it against a wall. He watched the flames leap swiftly up it for a moment or two, then grabbed his rifle and left.

Returning to his horse, he strapped down the saddlebags. Stella had been struggling to break free when Ned appeared from around the corner of the barn. Now he walked over to her and with one slash of his knife cut through the rawhide line binding her to the post.

As soon as he took the gag out of her mouth, she gasped, "I heard shots!"

"The damned nester wasn't at all hospitable."

"You *killed* him?"

"What choice did I have? He came at me. We have to eat, don't we?"

"Was . . . he alone?"

"He had a wife."

"What . . . what about her?"

He grinned. "She wasn't any more hospitable than her crazy husband."

She looked at him in pure horror, then noticed the glow behind him. It was gradually turning night into day. Running to the side of the barn, she got a clear view of the flames devouring the cabin.

She looked back at him. "My god! What have you done?"

"Never mind that. We're movin' on. Get mounted."

He grabbed her by the arm and flung her toward her horse. She almost went down but managed to regain her balance. She turned to face him, crouching, panting in her fury.

"I won't go with you!"

"Damn you!" he said, stepping closer and cuffing her on the side of her head with his open palm. "Mount up I said. We're moving out!"

Her ear ringing painfully, she turned about

75

dazedly, and grabbing the saddle horn, pulled herself up into her saddle. Her face pale, her eyes streaming, she pulled her mount around and rode ahead of him away from the nester's place.

How long Stella had been pulling herself across the ground, she could not be sure. Had it been an hour? Two hours?

When she had started the moon had been high above her, gleaming brightly through the pine branches. Now it was in front of her. Still, despite her growing anxiety that Ned would awake at any moment and discover her moving toward him, she did not hurry her progress. Pressing herself against the pine-carpeted forest floor, she continued to inch her way toward Ned's sleeping form.

Once she had managed to work her wrists free of the rawhide Ned had used to bind her, she had dug around in the pine needles until she had found a heavy stone that fit comfortably into her right palm. One swift blow with it, she was confident, would shatter Ned's skull. The thought of this did not dismay her. Indeed, her anticipation of Ned Larson's imminent death filled her with a bright eagerness. Never before had she wished so fervently for the death of another human.

Charlie Rooney, her late husband, had come upon her in a Billings parlor house she owned and ran, and had immediately decided he wanted her for his wife. It had done her no good to point out to the much older man that she was a whore who not only accepted her profession, but was proud of its considerable influence in history and of its designation as the world's oldest. In addition, she felt it gave her an independence of which few married women could boast. She had assumed such an attitude would appall Charlie. In fact, it only encouraged him.

As he told her with a good-natured laugh, whenever he could find them, he always preferred professionals. And since he could tell she would never take any crap from him, he felt completely at ease with her. The way he explained it, their match was an ideal one. No illusions on either side. An easy acceptance of each other's individuality and no reproaches from either concerning their pasts. Furthermore, if he ever broke that promise, she was free to pack up and leave him. To that end, he was willing to place a sizable amount in a Billings bank in her name should she ever feel the need to resume her former profession.

So she had come with him to his ranch, taken his name, and had found the old cattleman to be as good as his word. He was fair to his hands, and kind, even generous to her. His unexpected death had hit her hard. In Charlie and the Lazy J she had found a welcome haven from the random cruelties and injustices to which she had become hardened over the years. Since neither of them were bound by anything more than their respect and affection for the other, the tie which resulted had gone far deeper than either would have guessed when she arrived at the Lazy J on the old cattleman's arm.

A spooked paint, Charlie's favorite, had thrown the cattleman. His head had struck a boulder. He had died on the spot. She would always remember the empty, sinking feeling in the pit of her stomach when she stepped out onto the veranda and saw the three unhappy ranch hands riding up with Charlie's lifeless form draped over the paint's saddle.

A few months later, out of her pain and loneliness, she had let Ned Larson into her bed. In a few minutes she would rectify that mistake by crushing the bastard's skull like an eggshell. . . .

For the last five minutes or longer, the back of Ned's head and most of his chest had been hidden by the tree under which he slept. She kept her eyes on his legs to warn her in case he awakened. Within a few feet of the tree by now, she tightened her grip on the boulder in her hand and raised up onto all fours, preparing herself for the lunge that would bring her astride Ned, the boulder crashing down upon his skull. She moved still closer to get a clearer view of the sleeping man's head.

Ned was not asleep. He was smiling at her.

She jumped up. Ned did likewise. She lunged for him. He sidestepped her neatly, reached out and grabbed her right wrist, twisting it brutally. She dropped the boulder. With cruel precision Ned swung up his knee. It caught her in the stomach. Retching, she collapsed at his feet.

He stood over her, contemplating her with icy calm. Then he kicked her in the side. She flopped over. He bent and tore open her blouse, then ripped off her bloomers and tossed them aside. Dropping his pants, he spread her legs and fell upon her, grinning.

"Thought you'd never get across that ground to me," he told her. "What took you so long?"

Stella flailed at his head and shoulders. But he just kept on grinning, and bracing himself, entered her with a thrust so powerful and deep it stilled her like a blow to the head. She turned her head and struggled no more.

When he had finished with her, he stood up and looked down at her. "You didn't like that, did you, whore?"

"I hated it."

"Good. The more you hate it, the more I like it."

"Pig!"

He pulled his right foot back to kick her, then thought better of it. "What's that about the pot calling the kettle black?"

With fresh rawhide strips he bound her wrists again, then dragged her back to the tree. This time he tied her to it with such a ruthless thoroughness, she could barely move.

"If you have to go," he told her with a grin, "just do it in your pants. Then we'll see who the pig is."

She spat at him. He jumped back easily, then

returned to his sleeping bag. In a moment he was asleep again, his steady nasal snoring filling the campsite.

Stella swallowed hard and fought back her tears—successfully.

Two days later, they broke from heavy timber. Ned pulled his mount to a halt and with an eager nod, indicated the towering cliff blocking their path.

"Some piece of real estate, ain't it," he told Stella.

She did not bother to reply as she looked at the immense wall of rock looming before them. It soared almost straight up for hundreds of feet. Tall pines growing on its rim looked no more substantial than toothpicks. Clearly visible against the cliff's smooth white face, an eagle was drifting toward them in a wide lazy circle. Granite boulders, some as big as houses, lay at the foot of the cliff, a confusion of pine and bushes poking up between them.

Ned booted his horse toward the cliff, Stella following. She had no idea why Ned should be riding directly at this formidable wall of rock. But she was past asking him questions and had in fact refused to speak to him since he had raped her.

Reaching a screen of pine at the foot of the largest boulder, Ned reined in and pointed through the pines at a crevice in the rock wall behind it. At once Stella realized that this was how they were to reach the hidden canyon Ned and she were making for.

Stella felt panic, a desperate need to stall. Once beyond this towering rampart, she would be lost. Forever at the mercy of this animal beside her.

"We'll never get through that wall," she told Ned, at last breaking her silence.

Ned turned in his saddle to face her. "Found your tongue, have you?"

"Look what you did to my blouse," she told him. Reaching for her torn sleeve, she ripped it off. "See?"

He grinned at her. "It was a pleasure, believe me."

"You *are* a pig!"

Leaning over, he swiped at her, just missing. She cowered back, pulling her horse behind his. As he gentled his horse and attempted to look at her through the screening pine branches, she flung the torn remnant of her sleeve onto a pine branch. Then she spurred on through the trees and kept on past him. He overtook her, then rode alongside her to the boulder. When they reined to a halt behind it, she saw that the crevice was only wide enough for a single horse and rider at a time.

Ned started in first, then thought better of it and backed hastily out.

"It ain't that I don't trust you," he told her with a cocky grin, "but maybe you better go in ahead of me."

She kneed her horse past his and rode into the narrow cleft. The walls leaned uncomfortably close. The sense of confinement was not pleasant. The walls gleamed wetly from the water trickling out of cracks. She glanced up and saw a distant sliver of blue sky. It was the only source of light. Behind her, Ned pressed her closely.

Her only hope now was that Longarm wanted Ned so badly he would track him even this far— and would find her torn sleeve fluttering on that pine branch. She was honest enough with herself to know how long a shot this was.

But long shot or not, it was the only one she had left.

Chapter 5

Longarm and Santos dismounted to examine the tracks. They were imprinted clearly in the sand on the western side of the creek. Two sets. The horse in front was a big, powerful animal. Peering close at the tracks, Longarm pointed out to Santos the shoe's imprint on the lead horse's right front foreleg.

"See that break on the outside?" he asked.

Santos nodded.

"That's Ned's horse. A big chestnut, according to Stallings. The same mount Larson took from that cowpoke he killed."

Santos nodded, then looked up from the tracks at the ocean of grass extending from this little creek to the distant mountains toward which the tracks led.

"It will not be easy to track this man across so much grassland," he said.

Longarm nodded. "We'll need luck, and plenty of it."

He was as weary as Santos. Already they had ridden for two days, and this was the only sign they had managed to cut. And once again the old Mexican's words had served to bring a cold dose of reality to their undertaking. Tracking Ned across this prairie was not going to be easy, and their search for him and Stella would get no easier when they plunged into those mountains sitting on the horizon before them, their peaks barely visible in the distant haze.

Santos, Longarm had soon found out, was a superb horseman—as much at home on a horse as any Comanche—and as tough as old hickory. His face was a leathery map of deep seams and countless wrinkles, but his eyes were as sharp as a hawk's, and he still had all his teeth. In the morning he shaved the stubble off his face with a huge hunting knife, the blade's raw scraping sound filling the campsite. His chief vanity was his long, handlebar mustache, which he trimmed every morning with a pair of rusty scissors he kept in his possibles bag. Longarm guessed his age to be somewhere in the late fifties; but he could be off by as much as ten years, he realized.

Longarm reached for his reins. "Let's go, Santos. We got a long ride ahead of us."

"*Sí.*"

Later that same afternoon Longarm sighted a distant line of cottonwoods to the southwest, indicating a watercourse. At once he found himself looking forward to making camp that night alongside fresh running water. Longarm glanced at Santos and pointed. Santos grinned and nodded. He too was looking forward to the water. Maybe they would both strip and clean themselves off. The thought was not an unpleasant one.

They turned their horses to the southwest and urged them gently faster.

A few moments later, however, Santos reined in his mount. Longarm pulled up also and looked back at him.

"What's wrong, Santos?"

Santos did not reply. He had lifted his head slightly and seemed to be sniffing the wind, like a nervous antelope approaching a water hole. After a moment he slumped back and lowered his head.

"Do you not smell eet?"

"Smell what?"

"Smoke."

Longarm sniffed the air. Yes. Stronger than the smell of the fragrant, sun-cured grasses all about them came that of something more ominous: smoke from a burnt-out or still-burning ranch house or cabin.

"The smoke is old," Santos said. "But it still hangs in the air."

"Where's it from?"

Santos pointed to the northwest—away from the cool, beckoning cottonwoods.

Shading his eyes, Longarm searched the horizon to the northwest. He saw nothing. No smoke lifting into the sky. Only the dim line of the horizon melting into the cloudless sky. The fact that he could see nothing was not significant. On these high plains the smell of things traveled enormous distances. It was said that the Indians could smell a herd of buffalo from a distance greater than twenty miles.

"You sure it's coming from that direction?"

Santos nodded gravely.

Pulling his horse around and turning his back on the cottonwoods, he said, "Let's go, then."

An hour later they caught sight of something solid on the horizon. So far away was it that they could not be sure if it was one building or two. It trembled and shimmered miragelike in the heat. They kept on. About five miles farther on, as they rode out of a long swale, the barn materialized before them with impressive solidity. And beyond it the blackened ruin of a nester's cabin. Only the fieldstone fireplace remained standing.

The fire had burned itself out. No glow came from the charred remains. The ashes were white along the rim of the foundation. Yet the air was still heavy with the smell of burnt things that were not supposed to burn: clothes, mattresses, pots and pans, varnished surfaces, pillows.

As they approached, they heard the impatient stamping of the horses still in the barn. Riding on past it, they reined in before the cabin's black ruin. A large portion of the floor had collapsed into the root cellar, and though the faint, unmistakable odor of charred flesh hung over the cabin, they saw no bodies. All about the yard were black, burnt-out patches of ground where blazing cinders had landed.

Then Longarm saw the crib—or what remained of it—sitting crookedly on the ground closer to the barn. Santos saw it at the same time. Both men galloped over to it and dismounted hurriedly. Longarm was closer. He looked in, then pulled back in horror. A flaming shingle had landed in the crib. All that remained of its tiny occupant was a charred corpse. Santos crossed himself and went down on one knee beside the crib.

Longarm left it and walked over to the cabin and looked down into the black mess that remained. It was clear what had happened. As soon as the fire broke out, one of them had brought the babe out, then gone back in to rescue the other. But the smoke and the flames had overwhelmed them both, and the child was left alone in its crib, wailing, the flames leaping skyward just behind it. And one of the blazing shingles flung up in that tremendous updraft had fallen back out of the sky—and into that tiny crib.

One more instance of life's gruesome ironies.

Santos had wrapped the child in a singed blanket and was carrying it toward a small hillock behind the cabin. Longarm saw what he was about, hurried into the barn for a shovel, then followed after him.

Once they completed the sad ceremony, they fed the workhorses and the one saddle horse, let them loose, then spent the night in the barn bedded down on fresh hay. They moved out early the next morning, eager to put distance between them and the small cross on that hillock.

As they rounded the barn, Longarm caught sight of something dangling from a fence post behind it.

Turning his horse abruptly, he guided his horse over to it and reached down. It was a strip of fresh rawhide that had been tied around the post and used as a tether. A knife had sliced through it. Dismounting, he inspected the ground around the fence post. Boot heels had dug up the soft ground. Someone had been pulling hard on the rawhide tether, digging his heels in during the process. Trying hard to get loose.

Recently.

Santos had already dismounted and was searching the ground in a slow circle. He came to a halt and looked over at Longarm.

"*Señor* Long," he said. "Maybe you better come see this."

When Longarm reached him, Santos pointed to the hoofprints in the soft ground. Longarm went down on one knee to inspect the tracks more closely. There was no doubt of it. The small indentation on the outside of the shoe was as clear as a signature. These tracks had been left by Ned Larson, and that prisoner he had cut loose at the fence post had been Stella.

Longarm glanced back at the burnt cabin, his mind racing. The full horror of what must have happened here almost overwhelmed him. Needing provisions, Ned Larson had ridden up to this cabin, taken what he needed, then murdered the settlers and set fire to their place so there would be no witnesses. And it must have been Ned who brought the baby out into the yard, thinking the child would be safe that distance from the flames.

Santos had already guessed the same thing. Coming to a halt a few yards away, he pointed to the ground. "The tracks of both horses, they are deeper here. Larson take many provisions from the cabin before he burn it."

Longarm walked over to him and looked down at the tracks. "That's what it looks like, Santos."

Santos snugged his sombrero down angrily. "Thees man, *Señor* Long, I think maybe he is the devil come to earth. He kill as easy as some men drink whiskey."

"Easier than that, Santos."

Longarm looked in the direction the fresh tracks led. Larson was making a beeline for a low line of mountain peaks clearly visible now on the horizon.

Longarm and Santos mounted back up and headed out.

Once they rode into the heavily timbered foot-hills, the mountain peaks they had been heading toward vanished, and on the slick, needle-car-peted slopes, they cut no more of Larson's sign. Three days after leaving the cabin, they broke from a heavy stand of timber and found them-selves suddenly confronted by the mountains that had beckoned them on for so long.

Sheer slopes vaulted skyward. Pines clinging to them seemed no more substantial than toy trees on a toy landscape. Running from north to south, the enormous rampart appeared to be an insurmountable barrier. There seemed no easy way to scale it—and no way through it.

Longarm took off his hat and blew his cheeks out.

"We camp here?" Santos asked, shucking his sombrero wearily back off his forehead.

"Sure."

"Why not we go closer to mountains?"

"We're close enough, Santos."

The old man grinned. "You don' like the look of them mountains, hey?"

"That's an awful lot of rock. How many armies you figure could disappear beyond that barrier? And don't forget, we haven't cut any sign since we hit these foothills. Talk about lookin' for a needle in a haystack."

"Is no needle we look for. Is a woman. And a killer."

"I know that, dammit."

"So we give up. We go back. Let the son of a bitch live. Let him have the woman. I don't mind. Then I go south, back to my people."

"Don't get ahead of me, Santos. I didn't say anything about giving up."

The Mexican's teeth flashed in his swarthy face. "Good."

Longarm heard the steady pound of hoofs

coming from the timber above them. Turning, he saw McWhirter galloping toward them. Whooping when he caught sight of them, McWhirter cut his horse toward them.

"I thought I saw you two ridin' into these foothills," he crowed triumphantly as he pulled up alongside them. "But I had a devil of a time catchin' up!"

Reaching over, he shook Longarm's hand, then slapped Santos heartily on the back. The old Mexican was grinning from ear to ear, as pleased to see the kid as the kid was to see him. Longarm was pleased to note that Mac was no longer lugging two gun belts and holsters. His freckled face was still pale, in sharp contrast to his red sideburns and mustache. Longarm could only marvel at Mac's tenacity in remaining in the saddle long enough to overtake them.

"Hey, kid," Santos said. "You look like hell."

"Yeah, I know," he told Santos. "A good strong breeze would knock me off this horse. But I'm alive, I can ride, and I promise I won't hold you two back none."

"I'm glad you're here," Longarm told him, "but the doc was crazy to let you go."

The kid laughed. "The doc didn't let me go. Soon's he turned his back, I lit a shuck."

Longarm grinned. Hell, they might find Mac's extra gun useful, no matter how erratic it should prove to be. "Well," he told Mac, nodding to the wall of mountains looming before them, "you got here just in time to see what we got ahead of us. Ned Larson's in there somewhere, and we got precious little idea where."

"Don't worry. We'll find the bastard."

"I hope you're right, Mac."

They rode on closer to the base of the mountains and that night camped beside a stream tumbling out of a narrow gorge. Before turning in, they went over their plans for the days ahead. The thing to do, they all agreed, was to split up and skirt the base of the mountains, scouting any passes, canyons, or gorges that might offer a way into them.

The next morning Longarm followed the stream they had camped beside while Mac rode north and Santos south. They were to return to the campsite in three days.

A day and a half later, deep in the mountains, Longarm found himself standing in a shallow pool, staring up at the flaring veil of water cascading from a ledge so high it was out of sight. In front of him was a solid wall of rock. He turned his mount and rode back the way he had come.

He was building a camp fire in the ashes of their earlier fire when he saw Santos riding toward him from the south. Longarm fed fresh kindling to the fire as the old Mexican rode up and dismounted. He looked very discouraged as he walked toward the camp fire, and Longarm did not need to ask what luck he had had.

"Coffee?"

"*Sí,*" Santos said. He slumped to the ground,

sat cross-legged, and took off his sombrero.

Longarm threw two fistfuls of Arbuckle into the coffeepot, filled it from the stream and set it on the coals. Joining Santos by the fire, he offered him a cheroot. The Mexican nodded his thanks and took it. Silently, the two men lit up and waited for the coffee to boil.

"I think maybe there is no way through thees mountain," Santos said at last. "I try one gorge, and find nothing, just swamp and mosquitoes. I find a game trail that take me high, but soon I will need rope to go any higher. And my horse, he is very scared. Soon I am, too, and I come down. This is fine country for outlaws, I think. Better even than the mountains of my country."

"The Sierra Madre?"

"Sí."

"How come you're this far north, Santos?"

"Many years some Texans want to hang me. It is all a beeg mistake, but they not want to listen. So I sign on cattle drive with *Señor* Rooney. He down there to round up many longhorns. He know I run from Texans, but he does not care. He is young man then. Have much fire in his belly. I like heem. When he die, I am very sad."

"Stella said he fell from a horse."

"Sí. A foolish way for a man to die, *Señor* Long."

"Call me Longarm."

"If you wish."

"I wish."

93

"Yes," Santos went on sadly, "a foolish way for a man to die when he find such a woman. *Señora* Rooney, she is good for heem. She is tough like heem, and strong, and kind. I like her when first I see heem bring her to the house."

"You know where Rooney found her?"

"Sure, I know. Everybody know that. But none of us care. And she do not care. Besides, what does it matter? The past, it is dead. When I was young *caballero*, I kill many Texans. I like to see them drop. They no yell like Comanches any more after I shoot them. Now I am a different man. I do not kill Texans. I have even drink with some." He sighed and shook his head at this remarkable evidence of reform. "I am old man now. The fires, they are out, I think."

"I don't think so, Santos."

The old Mexican reached for the steaming coffeepot. "I hope you right. I need such fire if I find this gringo bastard who take *Señora* Rooney."

Longarm took the coffeepot from Santos after he finished with it and poured himself a cup. He needed a fire in his own belly, he realized. He was getting discouraged despite himself.

Close to noon the next day, Mac appeared, riding hard toward them. Longarm and Santos got to their feet. When Mac saw they had caught sight of him, he began waving something at them.

"What the hell's he waving?" Longarm muttered.

"I do not know, Longarm. But he is very excited."

When Mac got closer, Longarm saw what he was waving. A scarf or bandanna. Mac charged up to the camp fire before reining in his mount. The horse was close to giving out. Long tendrils of lather streamed from its mouth.

Flinging himself from his horse, Mac thrust at Longarm what he had been waving. The lawman snatched it from Mac. Stella's blouse! This torn sleeve fragment came from the same blouse she had been wearing when last he had seen her.

Santos took it from Mac to examine. "It is from *Señora* Rooney's blouse," he verified.

"She left it behind for us to find!" Mac cried. "I'm sure of it."

"Where did you find it?"

"A two-day ride north of here. I found it on a branch in front of a wall of rock goes clear to the moon." He paused to get his breath, then continued. "Soon's I found it, I dismounted and looked around. Couldn't find nothing—not till I checked behind this huge boulder."

"Go on," the impatient Longarm prodded.

"There's a crevice behind the boulder. It ain't very wide. Just big enough for a horse and rider. I'd already scouted more than my share."

"Did you scout this one?"

"I sure did. It sure goes in deep. And when I came out the other side, I found a trail. And two pairs of hoofmarks. Recent, too. So I came back here for you two."

"This looks like the break we been hopin' for."

Mac nodded eagerly. "We owe it to Stella. That's some woman. If I hadn't seen that sleeve, I would have ridden right on past that spot."

Longarm could only agree with Mac. Stella was some woman. There was no doubt she had left that trail marker for them.

"We can't go north, Mac, until you rest that horse. We'll leave first thing in the morning. We got some fresh coffee over there in the pot. Help yourself."

Santos handed the sleeve back to Longarm and joined Mac as he made eagerly for the coffee. Longarm slumped to the ground, resting back against a tree, and studied the torn sleeve. Leaving this behind had been a courageous and brainy thing for her to do. It had told them what they needed to know. Indeed, it told Longarm more perhaps than she had intended.

There could be no doubt how this sleeve had been torn. There had been a struggle. A struggle Stella had surely lost.

At the sounds of hooves approaching the cabin, Stella left her bucket of dishes and hurried over to the open doorway, wiping her hands dry on the ragged towel wrapped around her waist. Dixie and Concho hauled their horses to a scrambling halt, dismounted, and charged up the porch steps.

Ned pushed out past Stella onto the porch. He was naked except for his long drawers.

"What's the trouble?" he demanded.

"Riders!" said Concho.

Concho was a pale, pocked fellow with a knife scar running from cheek to chin. A lean, curiously twisted man, his uneven teeth were stained black from the huge gob of chewing tobacco that pouched his cheek. He wore greasy Levi's and a filthy red and white checked shirt under his leather vest. The night Stella had arrived, Ned had forced her to bed Concho. It had surprised her how difficult a task it had been. Never before had she so felt such complete and utter revulsion. As a result, Ned's generosity had not pleased Concho.

"They inside the canyon?" Ned asked Concho.

"Not yet."

"How many?"

"Three."

"Shit." Ned ran his fingers through his tousled hair. He was still unshaven. "You get a good look at them?"

"No. But we left Ralph back there to keep an eye on them."

"You three been expecting anyone to hole up here?"

"Hell, no. We're just as surprised as we were to see you." Concho grinned then, his black teeth like fangs. "Good thing for you we was such miserable shots."

"Well, if this here is who I think it is, you bastards better aim more careful."

"Don't you worry none," Dixie spoke up. "We ain't so surprised this time. Who you expectin'? That U.S. deputy marshal?"

"If that's who he is."

Dixie was not a clean man. Stella had seen him drop his pants behind the cabin, defecate, then raise his pants swiftly back up without a thought of wiping himself off. Dark, ragged strings of greasy hair hung down from under his hat brim. He had not yet slept with her, but according to Ned, he was looking forward to it. Last night Stella had told Ned she wouldn't stand for it, that he was not to pass her around to any more of this crew. Ned's response had been to slap her, hard.

Dixie shifted his gaze from Ned to Stella. As his pale, maggoty eyes crawled over her, she shuddered inwardly and moved back a step into the open doorway, averting her eyes.

Dixie chuckled meanly at her clear reluctance to meet his gaze, then looked full at Ned. "This here deputy comin' after you or after your woman?"

"Both, I'm thinkin'."

Dixie looked back at Stella. "Well, now. That gives me a real incentive."

"Whoever he is," Ned told him, "he dies hard. You better have more'n an incentive."

"I do. A sawed-off shotgun."

"You'll have to get pretty close to use that."

Concho spoke up then. "Don't worry. He will. I seen him use that."

"I'll be dressed in a minute," Ned told them.

He pushed past Stella into the cabin. With a sick emptiness in the pit of her stomach, she watched Concho and Dixie descend the porch steps. Longarm and those with him didn't have a chance. They would never get out of that canyon alive. Ned and these outlaws would see to that.

After Ned had established his identity and the three outlaws had allowed them up the trail out of the canyon, Ned had taken charge with a quiet, unnerving brutality that immediately cowed the gang into submission. When the third gang member—a fat bully of a man—had seen fit to protest, however feebly, Ned had beaten him with a thoroughness that had not been pleasant to watch. From that moment on there was no longer any question who was in command.

As Dixie and Concho reached the yard and mounted up, Stella turned from the doorway and started back across the kitchen to her waiting bucket of dishes.

"Hey, Stella!" Concho called in to her. "Bring us out some water!"

"Yeah!" seconded Dixie. "It's damn hot out here!"

She was about to tell them to use the horse trough, but thought better of it. Snatching two tin cups out of the bucket, she filled them from the sink pump and left the cabin with them. The realization that Longarm had found her marker and was on his way into this canyon had thoroughly unnerved her. She could barely hold the tin cups steady as she handed them up to the two men.

Without a word of thanks they snatched the cups from her. Stepping back, she watched them slake their thirst, water sluicing down their unshaven chins. These two animals must not succeed in killing Longarm, she told herself. And they wouldn't. Not if she had anything to say about it.

The two men handed down the empty tin cups. She snatched them back and returned to the cabin. As she mounted the porch steps, Ned burst from the cabin, dressed, his gun belt on, a Winchester in his hand. Without a word he brushed past her and headed for the barn to saddle up his mount. She watched him disappear into the barn, then hurried into the cabin.

But not back to that wooden bucket full of greasy dishes.

Chapter 6

The hard-packed trail Mac had found on the other side of the cleft took the three riders along the rim of a vast wetland, following a route that kept them close beside a rock wall so sheer no vegetation showed on its bald flank. The wetland was a dreary sight. All that met the eye were patches of swamp grass, low brush, a few dead pines, and cattails. Where the ground was more solid, willows lined the trail. At times, there was so little room between the willows and the mountainside, the flanks of their horses brushed the rock wall.

After more than three hours, they gained higher, solid ground and not long after, they were able to put the wetland behind them. It was Longarm, riding just a little ahead of the others, who first saw the yawning mouth of the canyon dead ahead.

He pulled up and waited for the others to catch up.

"They be in that canyon, I bet," Santos said.

"Or somewhere beyond it."

"And waiting," Mac finished up.

"That goes without saying," Longarm said.

Santos clapped his heels to his mount's flanks and surged ahead of them. Smiling, Longarm spurred after him, Mac following close behind. Santos was right. Now was no time for debate.

When they got closer, they saw a glacier-fed stream issuing from the canyon. Sandbars at its mouth split the stream into a northern and a southern fork. It was the southern branch that fed the marshland, while the other one, cutting a deeper channel, disappeared to the north.

They splashed across the stream and entered the canyon. It appeared wiser for them to keep in the shadows of the canyon's north face. The southern rim was considerably higher than the northern. Any rifle fire from that height would be futile and would serve only to warn them. They rode on deeper into the canyon, following the stream's twisting path through the canyon as it twice doubled back upon itself.

With each passing mile, the canyon's floor grew narrower, the stream swifter. It was soon brown with the silt churned up by the rapids just beneath its surface. At last the roaring, headlong stream crowded so close upon the three riders they were forced to cross to the other side of it in order to continue. Crossing the stream was not easy, but they managed, and a few miles farther on, after following a sharp bend, they saw ahead of them a well-worn trail cut out of the canyon's south wall.

Reaching its base Longarm reined in and dismounted. Santos and Mac pulled up alongside him and dismounted also. A quick inspection of the ground showed traces of wagon wheels and the pounding impact of many horses, clear sign that had accumulated over a considerable time.

Longarm took off his hat and mopped his brow as he lifted his head to let his eyes trace the route the trail took up the canyon wall. Once past a litter of shale and gravel, it led to a pine-clad ridge about halfway up, then doubled back, disappearing from sight as it ascended to the canyon's rim hundreds of feet above them.

Beside him, Santos nudged his sombrero back off his head as he too peered up at the trail. "I do not like that," he said. "We will be like flies on a wall."

"Ever try to shoot a fly?"

"Yes, that is impossible. But these horses we ride," Santos reminded him, "they do not have wings."

"Maybe we ought to camp down here for now," Mac suggested.

"Down here?"

"Sure, and wait until it gets dark."

"Climbing that trail in the dark will make it as tough for us as any of Ned's gunslicks. But there's no sense in borrowing trouble, Mac. Right now, we don't know for sure anyone's up there."

"Longarm ees right," Santos said. "They could have bushwhack us for sure anytime we enter canyon. But they not do this. Maybe we many miles from their hideout."

"You don't think we been spotted yet?" Mac asked Longarm.

"How in hell can we tell that?" Longarm asked, reaching for his reins. "Now let's cut the palaver and get on with it."

He vaulted into his saddle, then leaned forward and pulled his Winchester from its scabbard. In a moment his horse's hoofs were plunging through the gravel at the base of the canyon wall. Behind him he could hear Mac and Santos following close behind.

Mac was nervous. And he had reason to be. Hell, only a numbskull would not be at a time like this. But it did no good for any of them to try and guess what lay ahead. The only way Longarm knew to find out for sure if Ned Larson was up on that rim waiting for him was to ride on up and find out. They'd know soon enough.

Ralph Timmerman had been riding along the southern rim for the past two hours, keeping an eye on the three riders below him in the canyon. Aware they would soon reach the foot of the trail that led up to the rim, he had spurred ahead to find a good spot from which to blast them. He was hoping he wouldn't have to take them on by himself, that Concho and Dixie would soon get back with Larson to lend him a hand.

He tethered his mount in the timber behind the rim, then worked his way carefully down the slope until he found a good spot behind a boulder. It was about ten feet below the rim and gave him a clear view of the trail's last hundred yards. Anyone trying to gallop that remaining distance in the face of hostile fire would have little chance of making the rim unscathed.

Comforted by this thought, Ralph levered a fresh load into his Winchester's firing chamber and tried to make himself comfortable. This was not easy for a man as grossly overweight as he was. His patched, filthy clothes seemed engaged in a desperate battle to keep his swollen body from exploding. Picking his way down the slope a moment before had left him breathing heavily. His beefy face was round and hairless, his eyes tiny, and his flattened nose had large, hairy nostrils—porcine features that fit perfectly his hoglike bulk.

Removing his black, floppy-brimmed hat, he mopped his brow with his bandanna and leaned back against the slope. To ease his thudding heart, he closed his eyes and rested. The sound of approaching hoofbeats alerted him. The pounding hooves halted back in the timber. A moment later he heard booted feet crossing toward the rim above him.

"Hey, Ralph!" he heard Concho call. "Where you at?"

"Down here!"

Concho's head appeared above the rim as he looked down the slope at Ralph. A moment later Ned's and Dixie's heads appeared beside Concho's. They must have left their horses back in the timber.

"They got here yet?" Ned asked.

"It won't be long. I left them back down the canyon about ten minutes ago and galloped ahead."

"Get up here while we plan this out."

Timmerman stared at the slope he would have to climb and groaned inwardly. But there was nothing for it, he realized, and with a barely audible groan pushed himself out from behind the boulder and struggled back up the steep slope.

"That's a good spot you got down there," said Ned, grinning. "Think you can survive going back down again?"

"You want me to go back down?"

"Sure."

"Then what the hell did you call me up here for?"

"Don't you know, you big fat bucket of swill?" Ned replied, still smiling. "I like to watch you sweat."

Ralph felt himself shrink under Ned's withering contempt. For a moment he had visions of himself reaching for his six-gun and blasting the smile off Ned's face. But he swiftly banished such suicidal notions.

Concho stepped closer to him. "How far back

down the canyon would you say they were, Ralph?"

"Not far. Hell, they might even be below us in the canyon right now."

Dixie dropped the reins of his mount and hurried over to the rim and peered down. "I don't see 'em yet," he called back.

"They ain't far back, I'm tellin' you," Ralph told Larson.

Concho turned to Larson. "How we goin' to work this? We going to catch them on the way up, or while they're still in the canyon? We could bottle them up down there. It'd be like shootin' fish in a barrel. Nothing to it."

Ned shook his head emphatically. "No, we ain't that good a shots. They'd find places to hide. Then it would drag on. Too sloppy that way. We wait until they get up near the rim. Then we pick 'em off the trail like flies on a shithouse wall. They'll be a lot closer, and when we open up they won't have nowhere to go."

"Yeah," agreed Concho. "I like that."

Ned looked back at Ralph. "Don't open up until I do. I'll fire first—at that big tall bastard of a U.S. marshal. Stella says his name is Long."

"Shit," said Concho. "Did you say Long? Custis Long?"

"She didn't tell me his first name."

"If that's Custis Long, I know the bastard. He's the one packed me off to Yuma. He ain't

no one to mess with, Ned. They call him Longarm."

"They'll be callin' him Shortarm when we get
through with him."

Dixie was still peering down into the canyon.
"I can see 'em!" he cried softly, urgently.
"They's three of 'em, all right. They're holdin'
back, Ned. Looks like they don't want to climb
the trail."

"They will. There's no other way up here."

"You're right," said Dixie. "Here they come!"

He left the rim and hurried back to them, his
pale eyes gleaming in anticipation.

Ned looked back at Ralph. "Go on, Ralph.
What are you waitin' for? Get on back down
there. We'll take our positions farther along the
rim."

Ralph turned and worked his way back down
the slope, slipping and sliding awkwardly, fearful
that at any moment he would lose his balance
and go tumbling headlong. Behind him, the cruel
chuckles of the others watching him caused his
face to redden. It was all that damn Larson's
fault! Now Concho and Dixie were both picking
on him. Ralph felt like an unloved boy who had
been chastised and sent from the table without
his supper.

Reaching the boulder, he checked his rifle's
load, then glanced back at the rim. Larson was
taking up a position on the lip of the rim less
than fifty yards away. Concho and Dixie were
settling down out of sight farther down, Ralph

guessed. In a moment Larson had made himself comfortably flat on the ground, his rifle out in front of him. Watching Larson, the thought entered Ralph's mind that all he would have to do to take out the bastard would be to swing his rifle up just a fraction, center his sights on the bastard's head, take his time, and squeeze the trigger.

He was certain that Concho and Dixie would treat him as a hero if he took out this mean son of a bitch. And that would still leave the three of them to take out the three riders on the trail below. But what if he missed Larson? Just the thought of it terrified Ralph.

With a troubled sigh, he turned his attention back to the trail. He had a clear view of it as far as the last switchback. Nothing yet. No sign of them three riders.

Ten minutes later, he suddenly narrowed his eyes. The top of a hat was visible just below the switchback. He could see it bobbing slightly from the motion of the horse. And echoing clearly off the canyon walls came the clop of hoofs on the trail along with the unmistakable sound of loose gravel and pieces of shale sluicing into the canyon below.

Here they come, Ralph told himself, his entire body clammy with sweat. He wiped off the perspiration that had collected in his eyebrows, then eased off the safety on his Winchester and steadied it on the top of the boulder.

* * *

Less than ten minutes after Ned and the others rode off, Stella had saddled one of the horses in the barn and taken off after them. She was careful to keep well back of them as she followed them through the timber. They were not concerned about her in the least, however, and never once looked back. She took something else besides the horse with her when she rode from the barn. A pitchfork. Two of its tines were broken off, and the rest were rusted pretty badly. It wasn't much of a weapon, and she wasn't sure exactly how she was going to use it. But use it she would when the time came.

When the three men broke through the timber and rode out onto the rim of the canyon, she pulled up and dismounted, tethered her horse and moved cautiously through the timber, halting at its edge. Through a screen of pine branches she watched Ned and the others as they made their plans. Their voices carried well enough for her to hear most of what they said. When Dixie called out to the others that Longarm and his party were below in the canyon, she heard him clearly. A moment later she watched Ralph Timmerman scramble below the rim, the others laughing at the fat man's clumsy progress. A moment later the others moved off to find vantage points farther down the rim.

Longarm would never make it. Not with these rattlesnakes waiting to pick him off. It was clear what they intended. To pick them off just below the rim, while they were still on the trail.

110

But what could she do? She was only one person. And she didn't have a gun. Only this fool pitchfork. And the closest outlaw was Ralph Timmerman. She couldn't see him from where she crouched. But he was straight ahead of her, positioned below the rim. He would be waiting for Ned's first shot, she knew. And then he would open up on Longarm and the others with his rifle. At once she knew what she had to do and tightened her grip on the pitchfork's handle.

As Longarm reached the last switchback and turned his horse, he caught the glint of sunlight on a gun barrel. The gunslick was positioned on the rim just above him. Longarm had saved his mount for this moment. He slammed his heels into the animal's flanks and let out a howl. The horse leaped forward, its hooves sending gravel flying as it pounded up the trail. He could hear Santos and Mac behind him doing the same.

On the slope near where the trail reached the canyon's rim, a black floppy-brimmed hat rose up from behind a boulder. From under the hat a balloonlike face became visible. Longarm had never seen a face that swollen, that round. The gunslick raised his rifle and took aim. Wrapping his reins around the saddle horn, Longarm levered his Winchester swiftly and opened up on the fat man. The bullets ricocheted harmlessly off the boulder, but at least it kept the man's head down. At the same moment, rifle fire opened up on them from all along the rim. Like infuriated hornets, hot lead whined about them. Longarm spurred on, Santos and Mac keeping pace behind him. They were heading straight for that fat gent behind the boulder. But they had no choice. There was no other way to reach the canyon's rim.

Then Longarm saw an astonishing thing.

Stella appeared on the rim with a pitchfork in her hand. She scrambled swiftly down the slope and pulled up behind the fat man. He rose up from behind the boulder and started to turn just as she drove the pitchfork into his back. Above the whine of ricocheting bullets, Longarm heard the man's cry. His black hat went tumbling down the slope. He dropped his rifle and grappled feebly with her.

But there was not much he could do with a pitchfork planted in his back, and Stella was merciless. She slammed him on the side of the head with the barrel of his own rifle. He tumbled out from behind the boulder, turned in midair, and began bouncing down the steep slope like a rubber barrel. His momentum increased until he launched into space and vanished from Longarm's sight, the pitchfork still in his back.

Stella remained behind the boulder. Longarm spurred his horse on toward her. She waved, then lifted the rifle she had taken from the fat man and opened up a steady fire at an outlaw on the rim behind Longarm. Ducking low to avoid being caught in Stella's fire, Longarm galloped up onto the canyon's rim and turned in his saddle to watch as Mac and Santos clattered up after him.

"The timber!" he cried. "Make for the timber!"

They charged past him. Longarm slammed his Winchester back into its scabbard and broke back toward the rim. Lead sang past his ears. Dismounting, he leaned over the rim to peer down. Stella was about ten feet below him, still behind the boulder firing at someone she had pinned on the canyon rim farther down.

"Stella!" he cried. "Get up here!"

She flung her head around, saw him, and started to scramble up the slope. He went halfway down to take the rifle and grab her hand. Hauling her up onto the rim, he flung her onto his horse and rode hard for the timber. Hot lead slashed through the branches and thudded into tree trunks.

Once in the timber, he pulled up. Stella slid down.

Longarm dismounted and hurried back to the edge of the timber in time to see three men race from the rim and vanish into the timber. A moment later, he heard them riding off. The pound of their hooves faded rapidly. He turned and walked back to Stella. As he reached her, Santos and Mac approached, leading their lathered mounts.

Santos greeted Stella, a pleased smile on his parchment face, then he looked unhappily at

Longarm and pointed to the bullet hole in his sombrero's brim.

"Looks like you got lucky," said Longarm.

"If I am lucky, they no ruin my sombrero. This I have for many years. Look what they do to it."

Apparently unscathed, Mac paused in front of Stella. "I sure am glad to see you, Miss Stella," he said.

"Thanks, Mac."

"We try to take after them bastards," Santos explained. "But our horses, they are plumb worn out."

"We all are," admitted Longarm. "Never mind, though. We got this far, and now we have Stella to lead us to their camp. That so, Stella?"

She nodded and started to smile. But she never made it. Her face went bedsheet white and her smile vanished. She began trembling all over. Longarm pulled her close. Tears rolled down her cheeks. He felt her body shake as the sobs came. Only now, it seemed, was she fully aware of what she had just done, how close she had come to death. Perhaps she was remembering as well the feel of plunging the pitchfork into that fat man's back. Gradually, her sobs subsided.

"Stella," Longarm said gently, "you are one crazy woman."

"But I didn't have a gun," she told him, her voice faint. "I *had* to use that pitchfork."

114

"That's not what I meant. I meant you could have got your head shot off."

"But you and Santos and Mac could have been killed!"

He grinned. "Well, thanks to you we weren't. No need for you to feel bad, Stella. You did just fine."

She blinked up at him. "But all I remember for sure is running out of the timber with the pitchfork and attacking Ralph. I can't seem to remember hardly anything after that. It's all like a dream."

"That was no dream, Stella. You saved our lives."

Her trembling ceased. She pushed away to look up into his face. "Yes. That's right. I did. And that's all that matters." She stepped back out of his arms, her face brightening. "I'm all right now," she assured him, palming the tears out of her eyes.

"Stella, them three I saw duck back into the timber. Is that all we're dealin' with?"

She nodded. "Three men, counting Ned."

"Now, those odds ain't so bad," said Mac.

"Who was that gent you were shooting at when I neared the rim?"

"Larson."

"Good thing you didn't kill the bastard. I got to take him alive and deliver him to Billy Vail in Denver, don't forget."

"You must be crazy," said Mac, shaking his head.

"I think maybe it be easier to rope a whirlwind," said Santos, chuckling. His old eyes gleamed at the prospect.

Longarm rested his hands gently on Stella's shoulders. "You willing to take us back to their place?"

"Of course."

"Thanks. And as soon as we get there, I'm sending you back to the Lazy J. You've had enough excitement for one summer."

"Custis Long, you just try to send me back," she responded heatedly. "I'm going to see this through and you can't stop me."

She smiled then. It was like the sun coming out from behind a cloud. Stella had been through hell and might see another helping of it before they collared Ned Larson. But she had more backbone than twenty Ned Larson's, and Longarm for one was proud to be riding with her.

That didn't mean, however, that he wasn't going to do all in his power to send her back to her ranch. He wanted Ned. But even more than that, he wanted Stella safe.

Chapter 7

Santos cantered through the trees toward Long-arm and Stella. Breaking out onto the knoll, he pulled his horse to a halt and dismounted, then strode toward Longarm. "I don't like thees."

"What don't you like?" Longarm asked him.

"They are down there for sure. We hear them in the cabin. But they keep no lookout. We check the barn. No one in there. They are waiting for us to rush cabin, I think."

"Where's Mac?"

"Inside the barn, watching the cabin. If they come out, he will signal with two quick shots. Then he open up on them."

It was close on to dusk. With Stella showing them the way, they had cut through timbered foothills and across a parkland, almost catching up to the fleeing outlaws. Longarm had expected the outlaws to turn on them and attempt an ambush. But when Longarm picked up their tracks a few miles from the cabin, he saw they were making no effort either to circle back on them or hide their trail. They had continued straight on to their hideout.

So now Ned Larson and his two outlaw buddies were down there, waiting. The cabin was a low structure with few windows and a small front porch. The barn was off to the right, which was how Santos and Mac had been able to reach it without drawing fire. It was not much of a structure. Its rear wall had collapsed and the corral poles were rotting, allowing the outlaws' horses to break through it. They were visible grazing on the flat below.

Longarm understood why Larson and his two sidekicks had run to cover in the cabin. Built on high ground, it was set back inside a concave wall of rock that towered high above it. The rear of the cabin was close to the cliff face, which meant coming at the cabin from the rear was impossible. A frontal attack meant they would have to cross a long, exposed flat without cover. And any attempt to rush the cabin from the boulders on either side would expose the attacker to withering fire from inside the cabin. Their only course, Longarm had decided, was to remain where they were and starve the three men out. It was a tedious, unpleasant prospect. Longarm would have preferred to take on Ned and his two sidekicks out in the open.

Meanwhile, for that night's surveillance they would take turns watching the cabin from the barn. Santos would spell Mac around ten, and at two Longarm would take over for the rest of the night. As soon as daylight broke, they'd start pouring fire into the cabin, remind Larson what was waiting for him outside and how little chance he had.

He pulled Stella gently aside. "I'd like to talk."

"I'm listening."

Longarm halted at the edge of the trees. "I think right now would be a good time for you to pull out, Stella. You'd be safe enough with Santos as an escort."

"Longarm, I told you. I'm not going back until you finish off Ned Larson."

"Listen, Stella. All that remains for Mac and me to do is starve them three out. It'll take a while—a long while, maybe. When Larson does surrender, I'll clap cuffs on him and take him south to Denver."

"What about the other two, Dixie and Concho?"

"I don't have any warrants for them."

"But they tried to kill you. Who do you think was firing at you on the trail?"

Longarm shrugged. "Maybe they'll come out with Larson, guns blazing. I hope they do. It'll make it easy for all of us."

"I want to stay, Longarm."

"Why?"

"I need to know that son of a bitch won't show up in my front yard a week from now."

"That won't happen, Stella."

"You promise?"

He nodded soberly. "I promise."

She looked away from him, her eyes suddenly thoughtful. Her resistance to the thought of going back now to her spread was beginning to crumble.

"Look at it this way," said Longarm, pressing his case gently but firmly. "The Lazy J needs tendin'. Hell, that's quite a spread you got there, and the cattle I saw looked pretty fat and sassy, ready for market."

"I know that."

"Santos was planning on going back to Mexico after this, but maybe you can convince him to stay on as foreman."

Stella turned her head to look at Santos. He was hunkered down beside the camp fire, sipping a cup of coffee.

"I didn't realize until now how much of a man he is, despite his age," Stella remarked, frowning. "As far as I knew he was content to remain simply a wrangler."

"How'd he do as a wrangler?"

She smiled. "Excellent. He is a wise and gentle man. Under his care our horseflesh was the finest around. Charlie remarked on that quite often. He thought the world of Santos. But do you really think he would accept the job as my foreman?"

"Why not ask him?"

She turned and waved to Santos. "Santos, would you come over?"

The Mexican flung the remains of his coffee into the fire, stood up, and walked over to them. "What you want, *señora*?"

"How'd you like to be my foreman?"

"For the Lazy J?"

"That's the only spread I got, Santos."

"You sure you want me to do thees, *Señora* Rooney?"

"Yes, I am, Santos."

Santos smiled, obviously very pleased. "Then I would be proud to be your foreman."

"We'll need more riders."

"*Sí.* That ees true. But I know where there are many fine hands. They be glad to ride for Lazy J, now this Ned Larson, he is gone."

Stella turned back to Longarm. "I guess you're right. Going back is not such a bad idea after all. I mean, putting the ranch in shape and then seeing to the fall round-up. We'll have a large crop of calves to brand, I'm thinking. But just remember, Ned Larson and those two down there with him in that cabin are worse than cornered rats. They're cornered rattlesnakes. So you and Mac be careful."

"Don't worry, Stella. Our lives depend on it. We'll be careful."

"Well, then," she said, sighing. "I guess that's it, Longarm. I'll be leaving with Santos first thing in the morning." She glanced at Santos. "Will that suit you, Santos?"

"*Sí, señora.*"

The three walked back to the camp fire together.

Inside the darkened cabin Ned peered out the window at the barn. "You sure?" he asked Concho.

Beside him, Concho nodded quickly. "I told you. I just saw him duck out. The kid's gone back to their camp."

"Who took his place?"

"The greaser."

"If it's who I think it is, his name's Santos. He's an old beat-up wrangler. Ain't worth a pinch of coon shit."

Dixie pushed his head and shoulders up through the trapdoor. "You two ready yet?"

Ned turned away from the window. "Let's go."

He followed Concho down into the root cellar. Ahead of them, Dixie ducked his head and entered the tunnel on his hands and knees, holding the lantern out ahead of him. Concho followed, then Ned. The tunnel was damp and he was brushing against its sides. Cramped, squinting through the constant shower of sand and loose gravel that filtered down onto him, he could almost feel the weight of the mountain above him. When he allowed himself to imagine what it would be like if the tunnel collapsed, cold beads of sweat stood out on his forehead.

Ahead of him the lantern's light winked out.

Dixie had reached the end of the tunnel. Concho followed out after him, and a moment later Ned scrambled to his feet behind a thick screen of brush. He sucked the cool night air into his lungs and looked about him. His momentary panic had abated. All he felt now was triumph. While those poor dumb bastards were busy watching the front of the cabin, here they were, out of the cabin and undetected.

"You sure you want to do this?" Concho asked Ned. "We could handle that greaser in the barn and ride out. By the time it was daylight, we'd be long gone."

"And on the run."

Dixie added, "That's right, Concho, we'd be on the run and out a damn good hideout."

"Okay," Concho said, "but I'm warning you. That big bastard Longarm is bad news."

"You got it wrong, Concho," Ned reminded him. "We're the bad news."

They pushed out of the brush and kept going, moving into the field of boulders. They stayed within it until they came out behind the barn. Reaching the yawning hole in the back, they pulled up.

"The greaser's yours," Ned told Dixie.

Dixie lifted his huge bowie from its sheath, his pale eyes glinting in the dim light. "You want to come in and see me use this?"

"Just keep it quiet. We don't want the others alerted by a gunshot."

Dixie slipped into the barn.

• • •

Santos stirred. Was that someone outside the barn? Was the kid coming back for some reason? He grabbed his Sharps, left the window, and slipped silently back through the barn. Reaching the gap in the collapsed rear wall, he stood in the opening and peered out into the moonless gloom. He saw nothing but the sagging, rotting corral poles, and the only sound was that of a coyote yapping in the distance.

For a moment he thought he saw two indistinct figures melting into the night. But when he stepped down out of the barn to get a closer look, he saw nothing but shifting shadows. What ees the matter with you, old man? he scolded himself. You jump at shadows. He walked back into the barn and returned to the window. The cabin windows were still dark, staring at him like the eyes of a dead man. He shifted and got himself comfortable at the open window, his eyes focusing on the small porch. He found it difficult to imagine the three inside it sleeping like babes. Sure as hell, they were up to something.

His eyes kept flicking to the sides of the cabin. Even if the outlaws boosted themselves out the back windows, they would still have to cross an open area to reach the barn or the cover of the boulders. He rested the barrel of his Sharps higher on the windowsill. He hoped Ned and the other two snakes would try to break out.

His Sharps was ready and he was ready. It would be nice to finish them off before he returned to the Lazy J. Long had told him he wanted Ned Larson alive, but surely that would not be possible if Larson and the others charged out, guns blazing.

Santos leaned his left shoulder and then his head against the window sash. His senses began to drift. He was perilously close to sleeping, he realized, but his will to rouse himself was slow to respond. He blinked his eyes, then changed his position. This sudden movement caused a shadow that had fallen over him to shift. Alert on the instant, Santos turned. Leaning over him was a man he had never seen before. His eyes were as pale as moonlight; ragged strings of hair brushed his shoulder. His right hand was upraised. As it swept down, the blade of a bowie gleamed dully.

Throwing up his forearm to ward off the knife, Santos flung himself back away from the window, carrying his Sharps with him. But the descending blade was too swift, slid past a rib, and probed deep into his side. Santos felt something searingly hot explode deep inside him.

His momentum had carried him away from the window. As his attacker withdrew his knife and prepared to strike again, Santos, raising up onto his knees, swung his rifle like a club, its steel barrel crunching into his attacker's knee-caps. Dropping his knife, the man cried out and crumpled awkwardly to the floor. Santos flung himself onto the fallen man, snatched up the knife and plunged it into the man's chest. Not sure he had struck the man's heart, he withdrew the knife and sent it plunging back into the man's chest a second time, then a third. The pale-eyed man under Santos trembled fitfully, his arms and legs thrashing like those of a pinned bug, his eyes staring out of his head. Abruptly, his limbs stopped quivering and the back of his head dropped heavily to the floor-boards.

Santos took a deep, painful breath. A terrible fire was raging within him. Leaving the bowie's grip protruding from the man's chest, he looked away from the dead man's pale, staring eyes and searched the floor for his rifle. He had to warn Longarm and Mac that the bastards were out of the cabin. His vision wavered. Waves of nausea passed over him. He caught sight of the rifle and began to pull himself across the straw-littered floor toward it.

He was closing his hand about the barrel when he slipped into darkness.

An hour or so earlier, not long after Mac returned from the barn, Longarm had come awake, then sat up quickly. Stella was standing over him, wrapped in her blanket. When she saw he was awake, she lowered herself onto her knees beside him.

"I couldn't sleep," she said. "But I noticed you were sleeping just fine."

Longarm knew what she was getting at and smiled. "I need the sleep. Don't forget. I got to spell Santos down there in that barn later tonight."

"I was thinking about that. I mean about me going back with Santos. Alone. And leaving you here to deal with Larson. I don't suppose we'll ever see each other again."

"Like I said, once I get hold of that bastard, I'll be taking him south to Denver. Billy Vail wants to have a nice long chat with him. About that inside man who fingered that shipment."

"Yes, I understand. But knowing why you must go doesn't make it any easier for me. I'll miss you. Very much."

She adjusted the blanket about her shoulders and he saw she was shivering slightly in the cool night breeze.

"Get inside here," he told her with a smile, "where it's warm."

He flipped aside his soogan's blanket. She slipped swiftly into the soogan. He wrapped the blanket over them both and pulled her close. She pressed her body against his and sighed. He rested his hand lightly on her breast and leaned close to kiss her.

She pulled back. "Please...do you mind not doing that? I don't want that...not now. And please don't take it personal."

"Sure. No problem. Don't even think about it."

To his surprise, she began to sob quietly, her

face pressed into the hollow formed by his chest and biceps. He held her close until her sobbing quieted.

"I'm sorry," she told him. "I'm such a baby."

"No apologies needed, Stella."

"It's just that I've been used like a whore by those bastards," she said, her face thrust against his chest. "I still feel unclean. I *am* unclean."

"There was nothing you could do about it."

"I could have fought harder."

"Sure, and gotten yourself beaten to a pulp."

"Yes. That's the truth of it."

"So you allowed them to take you. You submitted. You did the only thing you could do. No need for you to apologize. Never forget that."

She sighed. "Thank you, Longarm."

He said nothing more, just held her close.

After a while she spoke softly, bitterly. "But what I can't seem to forget is that if I hadn't let Larson into my bed in the first place, none of this would have happened."

"Stella, we all make mistakes."

"But I should have known better. Every time I think of it . . ."

"You've already explained it to me," he told her. "No sense in going over it again." He pulled her still closer. "Now just lay quiet. Don't think about it anymore. It's over now."

Snuggling closer, she murmured dreamily, "Mmmm, that's nice. So nice. And you're so warm. Just hold me, Longarm. That's what I need now. The feel of your strong body against mine. Perhaps I can take some of your strength back with me."

"You're strong enough already, Stella. Remember this afternoon. What you did took courage."

"Not courage, Longarm. Anger, blind anger."

"Shh," he cautioned, holding her more tightly. "Enough. Get some sleep."

Her body relaxed against his. He felt the tension ease out of her. Not long after, her steady breathing indicated she was asleep. Longarm relaxed also. A moment later, with her lovely warmth enfolded in his arms, he dropped off to sleep.

Mac had just dropped off when a hard-driven boot buried itself in his side. The force of the kick sent him rolling out from under his blanket. The back of his head slammed numbingly against a tree. He fought to stay conscious as he stared up at the man peering down at him.

He was a pock-faced cruel-looking man with a livid scar that ran from his cheek to his chin. He was grinning down at Mac, his uneven teeth stained black from tobacco juice. He shifted the wad in his cheek and expectorated a black stream of juice, catching Mac on his forehead.

Mac wiped off the tobacco juice and sat up, his back hard against the tree trunk. The outlaw brought his foot back to kick him. But as it lashed out, Mac grabbed the man's ankle and twisted. Gasping, the outlaw toppled awkwardly to the ground. Mac fell upon him at once, his fingers tightening about his neck with a wild, surging strength born of desperation. The bones in the man's neck snapped.

Mac heard pounding feet behind him and flung himself around. Ned Larson was running toward him. Scrambling back to his sleeping bag, he reached under his saddle for his six-gun. His fingers closed about its grip and he swung it around, thumb-cocking and firing in one swift motion—just a split second before the revolver in Larson's hand thundered.

Mac felt a numbing impact in his chest. Breathing became agonizingly difficult. He found himself gasping for air. A window shade began to close down over his eyes. He blinked in an effort to clear his vision. But the darkness would not lift, and all he saw before him was a night blacker than any he had ever known and into which he toppled.

The two shots brought Longarm instantly awake. Yanking his .44 out of his holster, he flung aside the soogan's flap.

"My God," Stella cried. "What was that?"

"Gunshots. Came from the camp fire."

"Who is it?"

"I don't know. Maybe Mac's shooting at shadows."

That's what he hoped, but he didn't believe it for a moment. He pulled on his britches. "Stay here and keep down," he said, as he leaped up and ran through the darkness toward the camp-site.

When he reached it, he saw two bodies slumped on the ground near the still-glowing camp fire. He ran over. One of the outlaws was lying on his back, his face black and swollen, his eyes bulging. He had obviously been strangled. Mac lay on his side a few yards distant, close by his sleeping bag. Death was so recent, his legs were still twitching. A smoking six-gun was clutched in his hand.

Longarm straightened and looked quickly about him. The strangled outlaw had not shot Mac. Someone else had. Ned Larson. He and his men had broken out of their trap and were up here now. Prowling. Spreading death.

"Longarm!" shrieked Stella.

Groaning inwardly, Longarm ran back through the trees. The sound of a struggle came to him —Larson grunting in angry exertion, Stella snarling like a wildcat as she fought back. He heard something heavy and metallic raking flesh and bone, followed by Stella's startled, feeble cry—more of shock than anger. Longarm broke into the clear and saw Stella and Larson grappling in the darkness on the far side of the clearing.

A muffled revolver detonated.

Stella's naked figure crumpled to the ground and Larson melted into the trees beyond. Longarm sent a quick shot after him, then darted into the timber in a desperate effort to overtake him.

He crashed blindly through brush and slammed off trees until he found himself trapped in a gloom that was close to impenetrable. He could hardly see the revolver he held in his hand. Recognizing the futility of any further chase at this time and anxious to see to Stella, he broke back to the clearing.

Stella's pale figure was still on the ground where she had fallen. She had not moved an inch, and when Longarm caught sight of the gaping hole in her back, he realized she would never stir again. Gently pulling her over, he saw the brutal welts on her face and shoulders and a black, puckered bullet hole between her breasts. Her eyes were wide and staring. But they did not see a thing. From the shape of her silent mouth, he imagined he could still hear her crying out to him. That very day she had saved him. Now, when she had needed him, he had failed her.

He stood up. A distant staccato of hoofbeats came to him from beyond the timber. The sound faded rapidly.

Ned Larson had eluded him once more.

Chapter 8

Santos appeared on the edge of the clearing. He was unsteady on his feet and was using his rifle for a crutch. When he saw Stella's body, he sank to the ground, propping himself against his rifle. He looked miserably at Longarm.

"The *señora*, is she dead?"

"Yes." Longarm hurried over to Santos. "You hurt bad?"

"Knife wound. My side. Feel like some wildcat inside me." As he spoke, he continued to look past Longarm at Stella's still form. "Who kill her? Larson?"

"Yes."

Santos's face went hard. "He is devil, that one."

"He got the kid, too."

"*Madre de Dios*," the old man said softly, crossing himself. "This ees one bad night, I think."

"But the kid got one of them. With his bare hands. Strangled him."

Santos nodded wearily. "In the barn I too kill

the *hombre* that came at me. I kill heem with his own knife."

"Only Larson's left, then."

"And us."

"Can you travel?"

"Yes. But I hurt bad. Maybe this wound you bind."

Ripping a blanket into strips, Longarm wrapped them tightly around Santos's waist until he staunched the blood flow. The old man had been leaning against a tree trunk while Longarm worked. Santos stepped away from the tree. The effort caused him to gasp softly. A grayness passed over his face.

"You goin' to be all right, old man?" Longarm asked. "Maybe you better stay here while I go after the bastard."

"No, *señor*! My grandfather, hees horse throw him so he walk mile on broken leg. He tell me one theeng, treat pain with contempt. Now I think I learn how to do thees."

Longarm did not argue with him. Letting Santos rest back against a tree, he worked until dawn burying the dead. It was a sad, bitter task, and when it was done he was glad to put the graves behind him—and grateful for Santos's company when they rode off after Larson.

"There's no question," Longarm said, studying the tracks. "He's still riding that big chestnut he took from the cowpoke."

Straightening, he turned back to his horse and

grabbed his reins. Stepping into his saddle, he glanced over at Santos. The old Mexican had not dismounted while Longarm inspected the tracks. His old, lined face was gaunt, his eyes bloodshot. For the last hour or so he rode bent painfully forward over his cantle. Longarm hated to put him through this, but for two days now Santos, uttering not a word of complaint, had stubbornly refused to let his condition slow them down.

At dusk, after proceeding through a high pass, they found a stream for their campsite. Longarm did not allow himself to watch Santos dismount. It was too painful. He moved off to gather up firewood and was returning with an armful when he saw Santos sagging slowly to the ground. Dropping the wood, Longarm ran over to him.

"My legs," Santos told him, his voice rasping weakly. "They like water."

"I think maybe we'll camp here a while. Couple of days, maybe. Until you get your strength back."

"No. You go on. I wait here. I am no good to you like thees."

As he spoke the cool night wind brushed them, causing Santos's teeth to chatter slightly. It was clear he had a fever. Longarm looked up and around him, searching for a less exposed spot. He found it high above them under an overhanging rock ledge, a cavern deep enough to offer protection from the weather.

"Easy now," Longarm told Santos. "I'm going to have to carry you."

Lifting Santos onto his shoulder, Longarm was alarmed at how light the old man had become. He might have been lugging a sack full of dried-out branches. Shifting his burden carefully to make Santos more comfortable, Longarm toiled slowly up the steep slope to the cavern. He was pleased with it when he entered. It ran deep into the rock wall, offering excellent protection from the elements. A fire could be kept going outside the cave under the overhang without smoking up its interior.

He let Santos down gently, leaning his back against the cavern wall. The old man's eyes were closed, but he was breathing steadily, if faintly. Inspecting the bandage for the first time since he had wound it about Santos's waist, he saw that it was black with dried blood, which by this time had hardened it into a shell.

He went back down the slope to see to the horses and bring up their gear. When he returned Santos was still unconscious. He built a fire outside under the overhang, got the coffeepot to boiling, then returned to Santos. The old man was still unconscious, his breathing steady, but unusually rapid. Longarm decided that now, while Santos was unconscious, would be a good time to inspect the wound.

He was forced to use his knife to cut the bandage off Santos. A layer of putrid skin came off with the last of the bandage. The knife wound was a small, puckered mouth oozing pus and blood so dark it was almost black. The area about it was swollen and discolored and looked as tender as a boil. He explored the swollen flesh with his fingertips and found it very warm. He rested his palm on Santos's brow. The man's fever was now raging. Evidently, the infection stemming from the wound was massive and deep.

The wound needed to be cleaned out. That much he knew. But that was all he knew. He tossed the coffee out of the coffeepot, refilled it from the stream below, and while it heated, he cut clean bandage strips from a spare shirt in his bedroll. With his knife, he opened the wound still further. Dipping the bandages into the steaming coffeepot, he swabbed the wound out, probing deep, as deep as he could get. Twice Santos came awake, startled, a cry on his lips, but each time he sank back into a blessed oblivion.

Working swiftly, Longarm swabbed deeply until he had used three full coffeepots of steaming hot water and was bringing from the wound a much healthier looking crimson blood. He placed the blade of his bowie into the camp fire's flames, turning it slowly until it was white hot, then probed deep into the wound. Santos cried out, but did not open his eyes, and Longarm pressed it in still deeper, thoroughly cauterizing the wound. The stench of searing flesh filled his nostrils.

To bind up Santos's wound, Longarm used torn remnants of an extra pair of long johns. The old man remained unconscious throughout it all. When Longarm finished tying the bandage, he leaned close and rested his palm on Santos's forehead. He was not sure, but it seemed to him that the fever might have subsided somewhat.

Later that night, he heard Santos stir feebly. Flicking aside his blanket, he hurried over and pressed his ear against the old man's chest. Santos was breathing at a normal pace, and there seemed to be hardly any fever. Feeling a hell of a lot better about Santos's condition, Longarm wrapped him in an additional blanket and went back to sleep.

The snap shot Longarm had sent after Ned Larson had found its mark. Whining off a tree, it had creased Larson's left forearm, shattering it. Now, after three days of hard riding, he had turned back, determined to end this pursuit one way or another. He had realized he couldn't go on like this. He had to find help in a town out of these damned mountains, a town with a doctor who could set his arm properly. He couldn't do that with those two on his tail.

He had managed to enclose his arm in a crude splint fashioned from two pieces of deadwood he picked off the forest floor. His bandanna served as a sling, and he did everything he could to cushion the arm. Yet every jolt, every pound of his horse's hooves, seemed to communicate itself directly to his shattered forearm. And whenever he peeked beneath the torn strips of cloth he had used to bind the splints, he sure as hell didn't like the look of the puffy, discolored flesh over the break. It occurred to him that he had heard of men losing their arms after a break as bad as this.

That the deputy marshal and Santos were on his trail had become evident on the first day. He had paused on a knoll to give his horse a chance to blow, and glancing back along the trail he had caught a glimpse of his two pursuers riding hard after him. They were at least a half day's ride distant. Ordinarily, that would be enough, but he could not increase his speed with his bum arm. By the third day he had realized that it was only a matter of time before the two bastards caught up to him.

Now, he sat his horse high above them and watched them enter the same pass he had traversed earlier that same day. Keeping high on the slopes above the pass, he paralleled them as they rode on through the pass and kept on. At dusk they stopped beside a mountain spring to make camp. Hell, if they had gone any farther, they would have found the campsite he had used the night before. He studied their campsite to fix it in his memory, then rode off, keeping a high ridge between him and the stream until he found a spot to dismount and tether his horse.

By this time he was exhausted. His aching arm would give him no respite. It was worse than a bum tooth. Hell, he wished that was what he had: a tooth he could yank out. But what could he do with an arm that hurt this bad? Cut it off? He shuddered. The thought made him sick, but the crazy thing was that he was beginning to think he might be willing to try something like that.

If only this damn thing would stop pounding.

He built a fire and made himself some coffee. A simple operation usually, but it was made almost impossible by his infirmity. At last he drank the black, scalding coffee and slept fitfully until midnight. Awake, he threw aside his blanket and glanced up at the night sky. The moon was high overhead. A bright silver dollar of a moon. Good. He would need the light.

He checked the load in his Colt, holstered it, and set off down the slope toward the stream below him, the same stream his two pursuers had camped alongside. He reached it finally and followed it. The underbrush and thick growth of willows and scrub pine forced him sometimes to wade out into the swift, icy water. He came to their horses. They were tethered in a small clearing bordering the stream. He kept on past them and peered through a tangle of willows at the spot where he had seen the deputy and Santos dismount.

Only they were not there.

Where the hell were the bastards? Their horses were behind him, so they couldn't be far. He stepped cautiously out into the clearing and peered up at the mountainside looming above him. High above in the mouth of a cavern, he saw the flickering glow of a camp fire.

He frowned. Why the hell had they gone up there? Hell of a place to camp if you didn't have to. Making it up that steep incline could not have been easy. Were they expecting him, for Christ's sake? The thought momentarily unnerved him. Calming himself down, he studied the situation. He would have to climb up there, beard them in their den—as his son of a bitch of a father would say.

He took a deep breath and, hugging his broken arm to his side, started up the mountainside toward the dim gleam of firelight.

Santos was awake, aware that he was covered with fine beads of sweat. He sat up and noticed the new bandage about his waist. A dark carapace of blood no longer enclosed his side. Longarm had done something fierce and terrible to him while he slept. A red-hot cannonball was resting inside him. But the pain was localized, bearable. And he was no longer burning up with fever. Still his damp, sweaty clothes caused his teeth to chatter. The warmth of the camp fire, still glowing fitfully on the ledge outside the cavern, beckoned him.

He flung aside his blanket, got carefully to his feet, and feeling his way along the cavern wall, reached the fire and sat cross-legged beside it. Leaning close to the flames, he gratefully bathed himself in their warmth. He was reaching for a piece of firewood when he heard a stone dislodged below him on the slope. A moment later a small avalanche of sand and gravel started sluicing down the mountainside.

Someone was approaching the cave. No animal was so clumsy as to dislodge a rock, and he knew of no wild animals that would approach a human's camp fire so directly, anyway. He reached back for his Colt and withdrew it from its holster, then peered down the mountainside.

His old eyes struggled to penetrate the gloom of the moonlit slope as he searched for any sign of movement. Nothing. Whoever it was had probably frozen the moment he had dislodged that rock. Santos wanted to go back and warn Longarm, but he did not want to make any noise. Not now. Not while that bastard was below him.

Listening, like Santos. Waiting.

For Santos knew who it was. Ned Larson. Santos could feel it in his belly. And he, Santos, wanted him. Flat on his belly, he inched past the camp fire and slipped like an ungainly lizard over the lip of the ridge and kept on down the slope.

Flat on a boulder, Larson watched. The old fool, he thought. Here he comes. But where's the other one? In a moment that question became irrelevant as it became clear the greaser was heading directly toward him. The six-gun in the old man's hand gleamed menacingly in the moonlight. The old bastard had guts. That was for sure. But he was too old to take a chance like this. The old fart should have known better.

Ned moved carefully down off the boulder and flattened his back against it, gritting his teeth against the awful pain in his arm. In due course the greaser, still inching his way cautiously along the ground, appeared from around the base of the boulder. His head came first, then his shoulders. As he started to look in Ned's direction, Ned stepped forward and kicked the revolver out of his hand, then clubbed him on the base of his skull. Santos slumped facedown on the slope.

"How's that, you old bastard?" Ned hissed.

There was no response from Santos.

Larson bent over the unconscious man, relieved him of his knife and flung it down the slope. Then he studied the cave entrance above him. He had not shot the greaser because he didn't want to wake the deputy, who might still be asleep up there. He listened. Not a sound came from the cavern. So far, so good. He still had a clear shot at the bastard.

He looked back at the greaser. Should he give him another blow to the head to make sure? Maybe he should kick him the rest of the way down the slope. No. His tumbling body would make too much of a racket. Ned turned his back on the old man and moved out from behind the boulder to continue on up the slope.

He had taken only a step when he heard the sudden digging of booted feet into loose gravel behind him. Before he could turn, the greaser had flung himself onto his back, wrapping both arms about him in a ferocious bear hug. Struggle as he might, Ned could not rid himself of Santos, and the inexorable pressure on his broken arm increased until the pain was unbearable. Crying out in agony, Ned dropped his gun and made one last desperate effort to tear himself out of Santos's grasp.

But the old man clung to him like a tick. A portion of the slope gave way beneath his feet and both men toppled backward down the mountainside.

Sitting bolt-upright, Longarm heard the cry still echoing on the slope. He glanced over at Santos's bedroll. Santos was gone. What the hell? He grabbed his .44 and jumped up. From the slope below came a dim, scrabbling sound. He pulled on his boots and raced to the cavern entrance and looked down. Beyond a pile of boulders two men, locked together like battling scorpions, were crashing headlong down the mountainside toward the stream below. One of them was Santos. Who the hell was the other one?

He plunged recklessly after them, slipping awkwardly on the loose gravel, twice almost sprawling headlong. He was near the foot of the slope when he recognised Larson, on level ground now, disentangle himself from Santos and leap upright. Santos, unsteady from his long tumble down the mountainside, could only push himself up onto his hands and knees, his head lowered and swaying groggily from side to side. Larson lashed out with his right foot and caught Santos in the groin. Santos uttered a muffled cry and rolled away from Larson, both hands clasping his genitals.

Longarm was off the slope then, running toward Larson. The man heard him coming and started to turn. Longarm flung himself upon him and slammed his Colt into the back of Larson's head, doing his best to drive him into the ground like a fence post. With a weary groan, Larson crumpled heavily to the ground, then rolled over onto his back, his eyes blinking up at Longarm. He was clutching his left arm, his face a white mask of pain.

"No more!" he gasped at Longarm. "I'm your prisoner! Besides, I'm helpless! My arm's broke!"

"Don't give me that shit," Longarm told him, sighting on Larson. He cocked the Colt. "You're a dead man, you son of a bitch!"

"No! You can't do that! I don't have no weapon. I'm crippled!"

"I don't care."

"Hey! You want me alive. Remember? You need me alive."

Santos had struggled back up onto his feet. He planted them wide to keep himself upright.

"Let me wring hees neck, Longarm," he said. "I finish him for you. Let the blood be on my hands."

Hearing those words, Longarm cooled off. He and Santos were out of their heads, he realized. He couldn't allow that. He would not let this bastard's blood be on his hands or on Santos's. They were not murderers. And Larson wasn't going to turn either of them into murderers. Larson wasn't worth it. Besides, the bastard was right. Billy Vail had sent Longarm up here to bring Larson in. Alive. He was the only man who could give them that inside man working in the Pueblo smelter.

Longarm backed off and took a deep breath to calm himself. "Leave him be, Santos," he said, lowering his gun hand to his side. "No sense in soiling ourselves on this piece of offal. I need the bastard alive."

Slowly, painfully, Larson got to his feet, hugging his broken forearm to his chest. "You got it right, lawman," he said, his mouth twisted in arrogance. "But first you better get me to a town where there's a doc can fix this broken arm. After all, you're the one did it."

Longarm stepped closer to examine Larson's arm. Larson had slipped it back into the bandanna he was using for a sling. Longarm inspected the clumsy bandage and saw how the flesh around the break had swollen. It was too dark to see much more than that, but there was no question the man was in considerable pain.

He might even lose the arm if it were not taken care of soon.

He stepped back from Larson and smiled coldly at him. "Christ, Larson. I'm sure sorry I did that. You just wait here with Santos and I'll see what I can do."

What he did was return with a rope and tie Larson to the foot of a tree, winding the rope around him so tightly he could not move, making sure that the broken arm was immobilized in the process, telling Larson how much better he would sleep now, then leaving him while he helped the weakened Santos back up the slope. They could hear Larson's steady, bitter cursing all the way up to the cavern, where Longarm examined Santos's knife wound and decided it was maybe on the mend, though he had to wrap a fresh bandage around his waist, the other one having loosened during his plunge down the slope. That done, with occasional cries of outrage reaching them from the stream below, they dropped off to sleep.

Smiles on their faces.

Chapter 9

Three days later near sundown, they came on a played-out mining town huddled within the walls of a steep-sided canyon, its single street winding between false-front frame buildings. The town had a weary, done-in look about it. Alleys ran back from the street, some reaching as far as the canyon walls. As he rode on past them, Long-arm peered down their lengths and saw shacks clinging to the steep, clifflike walls. Farther on he glimpsed the entrance to a mine shaft and the skeletal remnants of a stamping mill, both nearly hidden behind mounds of slag that spilled clear to the canyon floor.

A saloon's multicolored window blazed momentarily in the lowering sun; the sign nailed to its balcony railing read, FOOL'S GOLD. A block down stood the town's single hotel, a dusty, three-story brick building with ornate gingerbread cornices. The town marshal's lockup, a small frame building a block farther on, sat next to the livery across from the express office. Glancing at the office as he neared the jail house, Longarm noted its sorry condition. A portion of the roof had already caved in. No stagecoach line any longer considered it worthwhile to run a coach to this town.

Longarm turned his horse into the hitching rack in front of the jail house. He and Santos dismounted, then pulled Larson from his saddle. Half out of his head, Larson cursed feebly when his feet struck the ground. Longarm and Santos escorted him up onto the narrow porch, then nudged him into the town marshal's office. The town marshal was waiting for them in the middle of his office.

"Howdy, gents," the man said. "What've we got here?"

"My name's Custis Long," Longarm said, brandishing his badge, "and this here's my deputy, Santos. You the town marshal?"

The man nodded. "Name's Ben Gunnison."

"What's this town called?"

"Bonanza." The town marshal did not crack a smile. A tall, lanky man, he had a long, sad face, a lantern jaw, and sleepy eyes. But in them Longarm caught a quiet, steely glint.

"This here gent's my prisoner," Longarm said, indicating the tottering Larson. "I'd like to lock him up."

Gunnison lifted his key ring off his desk and opened the door to one of the cells lining the rear wall. Longarm steered Larson into it, guided him over to the bunk, then pushed him onto it. Larson hit the unyielding wooden bunk, wincing slightly, then passed out.

"He don't look so frisky," Gunnison noted, locking the cell door. "Where's he hit?"

"Left arm," Longarm told him. "It's broke. Needs to be set. Is there a doc in town?"

"Sure. If you can catch him sober or when he's not at a poker table."

"What's his name?"

"Douglas. But he don't answer to that. We just call him Doc."

"You got a deputy?"

"Hell, ain't no need for a deputy in this town, not since the mine played out."

"What keeps you and the rest here?"

"Hopin' for a miracle." Then he shrugged. "There's some talk of copper ore left up there somewhere, now the silver's run out."

"I hope you all aren't holding your breath."

He grinned. "Nope."

"I'll be back with the doc soon's I can."

"No hurry." He glanced at the unconscious Larson. "That poor bastard don't look like he'll be goin' anywhere."

In the doorway Longarm paused to look back at Gunnison. "It don't matter how he looks, Gunnison. He's a killer."

"That so?"

"Take my word for it."

"Who is he?"

"Name's Larson—Ned Larson."

Gunnison shrugged. "Never heard of him."

"Consider yourself lucky."

Leaving the jail house, the two men stabled their horses at the livery, then walked on down the street to the Fool's Gold. The barkeep pointed out the doctor to them. He was playing poker and apparently sober. The poker table was wreathed in heavy coils of blue smoke. A few patrons were standing behind them, watching intently. Noting the intensity of the four players, Longarm decided Larson would have to wait a while.

The bartender did not have Maryland rye. Longarm took what whiskey he had, paid for the bottle and took it and two glasses over to a small table along the wall. He and Santos sat down without a word, too weary to say much. Longarm poured for both of them and leaned back to let the rotgut warm his insides. It had been a long, miserable three days.

At the beginning Larson had been cheeky enough and full of complaints, and Santos had been barely able to stay in his saddle. But at the end of that first day, Larson had become a sullen, pain-wracked brute clutching at his unset, broken arm, as vicious as a sick dog, while Santos was riding upright in his saddle, color in his cheeks. This pattern continued for the remainder of the journey to this town: Santos getting steadily better, while Larson continued to deteriorate.

There was an explosive grunt from one of the players at the poker table; then came the sound of chair legs scraping back. Cards slapped the green felt surface and two of the players, stretching to get the kinks out, stood up. The game was breaking up and Douglas appeared to have the largest pile of poker chips in front of him.

As the doctor cashed in his chips, the barkeep pointed out Longarm and Santos. A moment later, the physician paused by their table. He was a handsome man with a leonine mane of snow-white hair reaching to his shoulders and the shifting, yellowish eyes and hectic flush of a determined alcoholic.

"Understand you gents wanted to see me."

"That's right, Dr. Douglas."

"Doc will do fine."

He pulled a chair up to their table and waved at the barkeep. The man hustled over with a glass and a bottle of Scotch. The doctor tipped him generously.

When the barkeep left, Douglas said, "Put aside that rotgut Carl gave you. This here Scotch is from my own private stock. I had it shipped in here myself." He pulled their glasses to him and filled them.

"Thanks, Doc," Longarm said. "This here's Santos. My name's Custis Long. I'm a U.S. deputy marshal, and I got a prisoner in the town's lockup. I'd like you to take a look at him."

"A criminal you have apprehended, is he?"

"Precisely."

"What ails the bastard?"

"A bullet of mine broke his left forearm. He did a lousy job of splintin' it. It's badly swollen now and giving him considerable pain.

He's out of his head most of the time."

"How does the arm smell?"

"Bad."

"It might have to come off."

"That's what I was thinking."

The doctor smiled. "But maybe I'd better take a look first."

"Suits me."

"Of course, my services don't come cheap."

"I don't have any money. Not for that bastard. But my chief would like very much to talk to him, so it's important I keep him alive —for that reason if for no other."

"He is a witness?"

"That's about it."

The doctor looked back at the table he had just left. It was clear he was still feeling expansive about his winnings. Then he studied Longarm and Santos for a moment, after which he poured himself another drink, tossing it down like it was spring water.

"Finish your drinks, gents," he said, "and lead the way."

Larson was still out when they entered the jail house. After the doctor's inspection of his broken arm, he directed Longarm to arouse Larson and bring him to the hotel, where he had his ground-floor office. In a room adjoining his office, the doctor proceeded to set Larson's bone. He was not gentle. For Larson, the pain was such that he began howling in outrage. Longarm stepped quickly past the doctor and silenced Larson with a single swipe of his revolver that caught him smartly on the top of his head. Without batting an eye, the doctor continued to reset the bone. With that accomplished, he lanced the swollen, discolored flesh around the break and cleaned it out with gauze pads dipped in strong, smelly solution.

"What's that you're using?" Longarm asked.

"Carbolic acid and water."

"Why you use thees?" Santos asked, peering over the doctor's shoulder. "What does eet do?"

Without glancing up as he continued to swab out the wound, the doctor replied, "It's an antiseptic."

Santos looked at Longarm and shrugged.

The doctor straightened up to wipe his hands on a fresh towel he had laid across the foot of the bed. "It's a new idea," he explained patiently. "A doctor in England started it. Lister."

"Think it'll work this time?" Longarm asked.

"Might. This is a pretty bad infection, however, so I wouldn't want to make any promises."

With the gunshot wound cleaned out, the doctor closed the wound, bandaged it, then wrapped the wood splints tightly about Larson's forearm. Finished, he stepped back to unroll his sleeves, walked over to the dresser behind him and filled a water glass with his Scotch. He tossed it down and ran his fingers wearily through his snowy shock of hair. Larson, meanwhile, remained unconscious, though it was more like a deep sleep. His steady snoring filled the room.

The doctor opened the door leading to his office and stepped through the doorway. Longarm followed after him.

"How's it look, Doc?"

"Larson's a young man. Strong. He might pull through, all right. But I'll have to keep an eye on that infection. It might yet get out of hand."

"He owes you then. And I do, too. This means I've got a live witness. When he comes around, Santos and I'll take him back over to the jail."

"No hurry about that, Deputy," the doc replied, slipping into his frock coat. "As for me, I'm returning to the gaming tables." He chuckled. "It'll take me all night, I figure, to lose what I won today."

Longarm watched the doctor stride from his office, then walked back into the next room and closed the door behind him. Larson was still snoring. Santos was sitting on the bed next to him. He looked exhausted and at that moment Longarm cursed himself for not having asked the doctor to look at Santos's knife wound.

He told himself he'd see to it the next day.

"Why not get us a room upstairs, Santos, and then get some shut-eye. When Larson comes around, I'll slap him back into that cell."

"*Sí*," Santos said. "I am very tired."

Santos left and Longarm sat down on the bed next to Larson, leaned his back against the headboard and took out a cheroot. He had just about finished smoking it when Larson stirred and opened his eyes. Groaning, he reached up with his right hand to the welt on top of his head.

He looked at Longarm. "I was pretty groggy when I came in here. That sawbones finished with me?"

"For now."

"You the one that belted me?"

"With the barrel of my six-gun." Longarm smiled. "It was a pleasure."

"You son of a bitch."

Larson examined his left arm gingerly, probing the bandage with his fingers, frowning, seemingly amazed at how much better it felt. He pushed himself back against the headboard, adjusted into a sling the filthy bandanna that still hung around his neck, and rested his arm in it. Relief had gradually flooded his face. He was obviously feeling much better and looked like a man who had just had a miraculous reprieve from a hanging.

"Hell, that's some sawbones," he remarked. "I feel good enough for a woman." He licked his lips.

"That'll be a long time coming, I'm thinking."

"Do you now?"

Longarm wanted to keep Larson talking. "Let me tell you something, Larson. I figure you for the kind of animal has to pay for it or take it by force."

"That's how much you know," Larson snorted. "What about Stella Rooney?"

"Mention Stella Rooney again and I'll break your arm all over again."

Larson grinned, relishing the fury he had

aroused in Longarm. "And not only that," he continued, "I got me a fancy piano-playin' gal in the Gold Nugget saloon in Pueblo. She gives it to me every which way but flying, and she never made me pay for it, neither."

"I tell you what, Larson. I'll let you ride out of here a free man. All you got to do is tell me who it was tipped you bastards off to that shipment."

"You really mean that?"

"Sure, I mean it."

Larson grinned at Longarm. It was a wide, carefree grin. In that instant, Longarm realized just how young Larson was. He was reckless, wild, and thoroughly unconcerned with the results of his murderous career. He simply didn't care what he did—or what happened as a result, to him or anyone else.

"Shit, lawman, I ain't gonna tell you who that gent is. And if I did, you wouldn't let me go, neither. Soon's I started to ride out, you'd put a bullet in my back and say I was tryin' to escape."

Longarm tugged his hat down onto his forehead, swung his feet onto the floor and stood up. "Let's go, Larson."

"I like it better here, Deputy. That jail cell's bunk is too hard."

"Quit stallin'. Get up."

Carefully, favoring his left arm, Larson eased himself off his bed and stood up. "Where's my hat?" he said.

"In your cell, waiting for you."

Larson headed for the door, Longarm on his

heels, his .44 out of his holster, ready and cocked. They were in the lobby, heading for the door when an old woman brushed close by Larson as she headed for the front desk. Larson dropped his right arm over her head, crunching his forearm into her throat with such force her cry was cut off instantly. Spinning her around and using her as a shield, he backed swiftly out of the hotel, at the last minute hurling her back through the doorway toward Longarm.

Longarm caught the old woman before she struck the floor, then held her upright as the desk clerk bolted from behind his desk. The old woman, her face pale as death, was having difficulty breathing; but aside from that she appeared to have escaped any serious injury.

Leaving her with the desk clerk, Longarm dashed out of the hotel. He looked up and down the unlighted street. There was no sign of Larson.

Pausing in front of the hotel, Longarm pumped two quick shots into the air. The effect was dramatic. Despite the lateness of the hour, the street came alive with the pound of heavy boots on the wooden sidewalks. Longarm saw the doctor and his poker-playing friends push through the saloon's batwings, a steady stream of patrons following out after them. Before long the saloon was empty and a crowd of townsmen were circling Longarm. In the hotel behind him, windows were flung up and queries hurled down at men in the crowd. But of course no one knew for sure what was up as they stared at Longarm and waited for him to enlighten them.

Gunnison pushed through the crowd. "What's this all about, Long? What happened?"

"I need some men," Longarm told him. "Larson's loose."

"Is he armed?"

"I don't think so."

Gunnison turned to the crowd. "Looks like we got an outlaw loose in town. Keep an eye out for him. He's a gent with a bum left arm. If you see him, signal us with a gunshot and we'll back you."

"What's he done?" someone yelled.

"He's a killer," Longarm said, "a rapist, and a horse thief. Looks like a kid, but he's more deadly than a rabid rattlesnake."

"Well now," drawled the doc, his voice carrying far, "guess maybe you'd better deal me out of this one, Long. I already done my bit."

He turned and headed back into the saloon, his fellow card players with him. Others followed him back into the saloon as well. Before long the crowd had shrunk to four men.

"I'm making you four my deputies," Gunnison told them. "You don't need badges and I'll swear you in later. This guy Larson's in town here somewhere, but he's got a bum left arm and he ain't goin' nowhere till he gets a horse. So let's go."

"Get him alive if you can. He's a witness and I need his testimony."

159

"We ain't goin' to promise nothin' along them lines," Gunnison told Longarm.

"I understand."

Two of the four men ducked into the alleys while the other two remained with Gunnison and started down the street, guns drawn, searching the shadows for any crouching figure. Longarm was about to go back inside for Santos when the old man charged out of the hotel, his gun belt strapped on and carrying his Sharps.

Santos had already guessed what the commotion was all about. Longarm filled him in quickly.

"I say we try the livery," Santos said.

"Just what I was thinking."

They trotted past Gunnison and his men, reached the livery stable, and ducked inside. They found the hostler crumpled against the side of a stall, unconscious from a blow to the head. They had guessed right.

Longarm was about to send a shot into the air to signal Gunnison when Larson, astride his chestnut, burst out of the shadows at the back of the barn and thundered toward them. Santos, directly in the horse's path, flung up his rifle and fired, but the shot went wild as the big horse slammed into him, trampled him, and kept on. Longarm snapped off a shot as Larson galloped past, but the shot had no effect, and Larson, head down, continued on out of the barn and disappeared into the night.

Longarm knelt by Santos. He heard distant

shots as others tried to bring Larson down, but he paid no heed. His attention was riveted on Santos. The old man was unconscious. A hoof had sliced into the side of his head, opening it up to an alarming extent. Blood poured from the earlier knife wound in his side. The horse must have stomped him there as well, Longarm realized miserably.

Gunnison appeared in the stable doorway, breathing hard.

"Get the doc," said Longarm, lifting Santos in his arms. "Tell him I'm bringing Santos over to his office in the hotel."

"We missed Larson. He got away, heading south."

"Never mind him," Longarm said, brushing quickly past Gunnison. "Get the doc."

With a sigh, the doc quietly pulled the sheet up over the dead man's face and turned to look at Longarm. "If it is any comfort, Santos was dead the moment that first hoof struck him. He didn't feel a thing."

"Tell me, Doc, how far and how fast can Larson ride with that arm of his?"

"Not far and not very fast. He probably felt so much better after I lanced his arm, he has no idea how weak he really is. I can't be sure I've succeeded in clearing up that infection. If I haven't, he'll feel it before long."

Longarm took out his pouch of silver. "If I

don't get back in a couple of days, take care of Santos's burial for me, will you?"

"Keep your money, Longarm. No need to pay me. And allow me to offer you my sincere condolences."

Longarm said nothing as he looked back at the still form on the doc's table. He had only known Santos a short while, but he had come to like him. He was tough, uncomplaining. A good man to ride with. Longarm would miss him.

"Thanks, Doc. Looks like I got some riding to do."

"Good luck," the doctor said. "I hope you catch the bastard."

"I will, if I have to track him clear to hell," Longarm said quietly.

He clapped on his hat and left the office.

A day later he cut Larson's sign and from what he could gather, the doc was right. Larson's pace had slowed considerably. Longarm knew what weapons Larson was packing. He had stolen the hostler's six-gun and knife. But he had no rifle. As he gradually overtook the outlaw a day after he first cut his sign, this fact gave him some comfort.

But not much.

He was following Larson's trail through a narrow canyon when he heard the sudden clatter of hoofs coming at him from around the next bend. He dismounted, pulled his horse closer to the canyon wall, and drew his .44. A second later, Larson's big chestnut thundered past him. The saddle was empty. As Longarm left the canyon wall to peer after it, Larson stepped swiftly up behind him and slammed his revolver down onto Longarm's skull.

Longarm's head exploded like a Chinese New Year as he sank to one knee. He tried to raise his gun. It was heavier than an anvil. Larson stepped close and kicked it out of his hand. Then he kicked Longarm in the side of his face. It caught his cheekbone and sent him flying. When he came down, the back of his head slammed hard against a projecting boulder. This second blow to the head did it. All the lines were down. Barely conscious, he could not move a muscle.

Grinning, his left arm resting in his sling, Larson strode toward him. He looked slightly unsteady, his eyes wild.

"I'm going to kill you slow," he said to Longarm. "I got it all planned."

Larson pulled up and looked down at him. He was more than a little unsteady on his feet. He weaved like a drunk man. His face was flushed, feverish.

"You won't last much longer, Larson," Longarm told him, "if you don't get back to that doctor. Ain't you noticed it? You're a dying man."

"No. You got it wrong. You're the one that's dying."

"Think back. Have you felt your arm lately? It's on fire, ain't it? You're going to have to get it lanced a second time, cleaned out again. You were a fool to break out before you were mended proper."

"Get up. I got something waiting for you."

"You're out of your head, Larson."

"Maybe so," he admitted cockily. "I do feel sort of funny. Like maybe I'm drunk some. But I'm going to watch you die before I head back to that doc."

"You're talkin' crazy. The town marshal will lock you up soon's you ride in."

"He ain't got nothin' on me."

"Santos is dead. You killed him."

"That so? Well, ain't that too bad. I hate greasers. Served the old bastard right. Now get up, I said."

Longarm found he could move his limbs now. But sitting up was another matter. His head was still rocking.

Larson stuck his revolver into Longarm's face and grinned. "Make a move, why don't you? Give me an excuse to blow your head off."

"Easy," said Longarm. "I'm getting up. Just take it easy."

Moving back unsteadily, Larson straightened and watched carefully as Longarm managed to get his feet under him and stand up. The canyon walls spun crazily about his head for a moment before they settled into their proper places. Longarm took a deep breath.

Larson said, "Move on by me. And don't try anything, you bastard."

Longarm said nothing. His head down, he

shuffled groggily past Larson, his right hand massaging the lump on the back of his head.

Larson followed.

Ahead of him Longarm saw the deep, concave hollow which had been scoured out of the canyon wall by the roaring spring torrents that careened through this canyon. When he got close enough, he saw what Larson meant when he said he had something waiting for him.

Somehow, using only his right hand, Larson had managed to loop two ropes over a couple of rocky spikes protruding above the cavern's entrance. His intention was to hang Longarm from his thumbs. Larson was right. If he had his way, Longarm would take a long time to die.

Halfway across the canyon, Longarm paused suddenly, as if he were finding it difficult to remain upright. He rocked unsteadily back on his feet and again reached up to the lump on his head.

"Come on!" Larson cried impatiently. "Keep movin'."

As Larson spoke, Longarm felt the man's breath on the back of his neck. He was that close. Longarm spun completely around to his left, his lead arm brushing aside the revolver in Larson's hand, his right fist slamming into Larson's face. Larson's revolver detonated, the round taking a piece out of Longarm's frock coat. Larson reeled back from the force of Longarm's punch. Longarm kept after him, grabbed his right wrist and twisted. The gun dropped to the ground.

Still holding Larson's right wrist, Longarm brought his knee up into his groin. Larson doubled up, retching. Longarm kicked him again, this time in the stomach, the blow strong enough to flip him over onto his back.

Longarm stepped back and waited. Rolling over, Larson reached out for the gun with his good right hand. Longarm waited. Larson snatched up the revolver, thumb-cocked, and swung around to face Longarm. Longarm had seen enough. He stepped forward swiftly and kicked the revolver out of Larson's grasp. Then he grabbed Larson by the left hand and hauled him upright.

Larson howled bloody murder. Tears of pain gushed from his eyes. He flipped about like a beached fish, his eyes bulging, his mouth twisting with the pain.

"My arm!" he gasped. "My arm."

Still holding on to Larson's left wrist, Longarm dragged him over the rocks and up into the cavern. By the time they reached it, Larson had passed out from the excruciating pain. Inspecting Larson's work, Longarm acknowledged that the outlaw had worked with devilish skill. To the ends of the rope, he had attached the rawhide strips to be wound about each thumb, and had already spread the sand carefully over the rock's surface under the rope.

Longarm tied the rawhide securely about the joint in Larson's right-hand thumb. Then he hauled up the unconscious man's broken arm and tied Larson's other thumb to the rawhide. Stepping back, he inspected his work. Larson's feet barely touched the sandy caprock beneath him, while the entire weight of his body strained his two thumbs.

Longarm waited patiently for Larson to open his eyes.

"Hey!" he gasped. "You can't do this!"

"Why can't I?"

Larson was panting from the pain, but had managed to raise himself up onto his tiptoes to take some of the weight off his two thumbs. His right foot had slipped on the sand only once. So far.

"You need me! I'm the only one can tell you who it was tipped us off to that shipment."

"I don't need you, Larson."

"You do!"

"You already told me what I need to know."

"I never told you nothin'!"

Longarm smiled and stepped back.

"You can't do this! You're a lawman!"

Turning around, Longarm picked his way carefully down to the canyon floor, Larson's foul rush of invectives following after him every inch of the way. Raw sewage gushing from an open sewer line. A moment later, astride his mount, he heard Larson's curses turn to sharp, terrible cries that ricocheted off the canyon walls.

Longarm kept going and did not look back.

Chapter 10

They'd changed the name of the Gold Nugget to The Lucky Lady. Once inside, Longarm recognized the layout, but everything else had been transformed completely. Still a very bad piano player, Amber Lane was up on the platform pounding away, singing about a lonesome cowboy or whatever, when she caught sight of Longarm striding toward the bar. She ended her song as quickly as she could, snatched her drink off the piano, and joined him.

Instantly, Longarm became the center of attention. Wherever Amber went the spotlight was sure to follow. The saloon might have changed, but not Amber Lane. Her jet black hair cascaded down the back of her red velvet dress. Her eyes were green, sending off a hectic sparkle as always, her prominent cheekbones heavily rouged, her full, scarlet lips mobile and expressive. She was all woman. Too much woman for some. Just right for Longarm.

"Hey, you great big drink of water," Amber said throatily. "Where in hell have you been?"

"Here, there, and everywhere."

"You still a lawman?"

"It's the best paying job I could find, considering my talents."

"How long you in town for?"

"That depends."

"On me?"

"Maybe."

"Jesus, let's find a table. What are you drinking? The usual?"

He nodded.

"Biff," she said to the bartender, "have one of the girls bring over a bottle of Maryland rye and two glasses. Put it on my tab."

"Sure thing, Miss Amber."

Her arm in his, Amber Lane escorted Longarm over to a private table away from the common people in a quiet alcove behind an ornate railing. The lamp on the table was a Tiffany.

"How do you like the place?" she asked, leaning back to look up at him as he pushed the chair under her. Her perfume was familiar, recalling other times, other nights.

He sat down and looked around the saloon. It made him giddy. "Just give me a few minutes," he told her.

The wallpaper was extravagant, featuring dramatic broad, black and white bars in a vertical pattern. The gaslight fixtures were highly polished brass, the light shades various shades of red. The carpeting in the gaming room to the rear was also deep maroon, contrasting sharply with the green felt on the gaming tables. The few paintings left on the walls were landscapes, the frames ornate and gilded. Gone were the fullsome, full-bodied damsels cavorting in streams and hillsides.

He took two cheroots from his inside coat pocket and gave her one. "I noticed the new wallpaper and lamps first thing when I came in. Sure is different than it was."

"But do you like it?"

"Of course."

"Why?"

"It's more . . . elegant."

"Yes! Exactly! Oh, I'm so glad you like it." She leaned forward so Longarm could light her cheroot. "I did the interior design myself. It felt so good to get rid of that drab wallpaper, the ugly furnishings, especially those oversized, silly paintings."

"There's some that will miss 'em."

"For God's sake, Longarm. No man likes women that big."

"So you say."

"I ought to know," she said, winking. "It's breasts a man wants, not great moon-sized backsides."

"This place has a new owner?"

"Yep."

"Who?"

"Who do you think?" She lifted her head proudly.

"Amber, you're coming up in the world."

"A lady of property."

"How'd you get a liquor license?"

"You mean with my colorful reputation?"

He nodded.

"I have me a silent partner. He's in for twenty-five percent of the gross, and he pays off the right people." She shrugged. "That's standard, Longarm."

"I suppose so."

He leaned back. It was like old times. Or maybe it wasn't. When he had enjoyed the pleasure of Amber Lane's company in the past, she had been just the saloon's singer and main attraction. Now she was a businesswoman. He wondered if this would change her any. He studied her and decided he should relax. Nothing could change Amber.

They had had good times together. She was tough, yet good-hearted. There was no nonsense about her. She didn't play games and she called it as she saw it and took good care of the men she befriended. She didn't much like women. Called them ungrateful cats. Men, she insisted, were more honest. Brutally honest sometimes, but honest, all the same.

Their Maryland rye arrived. He poured. They raised their glasses in a toast.

"To old times," Longarm said.

"And better times ahead."

"I'll drink to that."

When Longarm put down his glass, he pulled on his cheroot for a moment or two, studying

171

Amber as he did so, trying to imagine her with Ned Larson.

"Out with it, Longarm," she said, reading his mind as always. "You got business in this neck of the woods. Speak up."

"Amber, you ever know a wild kid named Larson. Ned Larson?"

The color left her face. "I knew the son of a bitch. Yes."

"He says you and he were good friends."

"He's a goddamned liar. I hate the bastard. He took it from me, Longarm. That son of a bitch took it from me, and all the time I'd thought he was just a sweet kid needed looking after."

"Some kid."

"Is he why you're down here?"

"He was arrested in Montana Territory a few weeks back. One of our men was bringing him back to the Denver office when he got loose. Larson's left a bloody trail since."

"You think he's back here?"

"Larson was part of the gang that attempted that silver heist a few months ago. They didn't get away with anything, but the bastards knew which unmarked car was transporting the silver. That means someone in the smelter here tipped them off."

"And you want the tipster."

"I don't know who he is. But my hunch is Larson will end up here, looking for him. He needs a stake and a place to hide."

"You mean he'll show up here? In my saloon?"

"That's how I figure it."

She groaned softly. "And when he does, you'll be waiting." She looked unhappily about her. "Please, Longarm. Don't try anything in here. This is all new furniture. That wallpaper cost a fortune and the bar came all the way from Boston."

"And that's a nice mirror you got, too."

"I'm pleading with you, Longarm. Don't wreck my place."

"Relax. Like I said, this is just a hunch. Larson may never show."

She leaned back, taking that in. It calmed her down some. Then she smiled. "Meanwhile, Longarm, you're always welcome to stay in my place."

"Where's that?"

"I got an apartment upstairs. If you think this is nice, you ought to see it."

"That's real generous of you, Amber."

"Nonsense. You know you're always welcome, Longarm. You're a rarity in this country. A gentleman."

"My gear's at the hotel. The Bennington. I'll have to go back for it."

She leaned forward and winked. "I can hardly wait."

A shadow fell over their table. Longarm turned to see a handsome, swarthy gent coming to a halt on the other side of the railing. He was decked out in a yellow vest, checked pants, and a long tailcoat. He doffed his fashionable, narrow-brimmed felt hat, and bowed gallantly to Amber.

"Just thought I'd drop in," he told her. "See how things are going."

"Custis," Amber said, "this here is Wes Longbranch. He's the silent partner I mentioned. You might say that mahogany bar over there is his prime contribution."

"I would hope I have contributed more than that, Amber."

She laughed easily. "Of course you have, Wes. Without you, I wouldn't have a liquor license. Wes, this here is Custis Long, a good friend of mine. We go back a ways, as they say. He'll be stayin' with me."

"Pleased to meet you, Custis," said Wes. "Are you new in town?"

"Just got in."

"Welcome to Pueblo."

"Thanks, Wes."

With a quick good-bye to them, Wes patted his hat back on, left them and sauntered over to the bar.

"Is he hard to deal with?" Longarm asked.

Amber chuckled. "He's a man, isn't he?"

Longarm finished his drink and was getting set to leave when Amber reached over and placed her hand on his wrist. "Longarm," she said, "would that man you're looking for likely be working inside the smelter?"

"That's the way I figure it. How else would he have been able to tip off that gang?"

"Ever since you came in, that fellow over there has been watching you."

"You know him?"

"He's a regular. Name's Barton."

"Where's he work?"

"In the smelter. In shipping, if I'm not mistaken."

"He might be our man, Amber."

"You going to arrest him?"

"How can I? I got no proof he tipped off anybody. That's why I need Larson to show. If he walks in here and throws in with Barton, I'll have all the proof I need. Until then, I got nothing."

"That might mean a long wait."

"Yep."

She sighed happily. "Well, then, I won't complain."

Longarm smiled and patted her hand. Barton was a short, scrawny man with a bald head so shiny it looked as if he had polished it. He was nursing a whiskey and water and kept his eyes on the glass—when he wasn't glancing up at Longarm, that is.

Longarm pushed his chair back and got to his feet. "Guess I'll go get my gear," he told Amber.

She smiled impishly up at him. "Hurry. I'll be keeping the bed warm."

In front of the Bennington Hotel, Longarm put down his carpetbag and looked for a hacky. He was about to raise his hand to hail one when he felt the muzzle of a revolver being pressed into the small of his back. He glanced back. It was Barton.

"Just pick up your carpetbag and walk on

down the street," he said. "And don't try nothin', or this here'll go off."

Longarm did precisely as Barton said. He could tell from the slight tremor in the man's voice that he was exceedingly nervous; and judging from the pall of whiskey that hung over him, it was clear his courage had come from a bottle. And was just about as reliable.

As they approached an alley, Barton said, "Down here."

The alley stank of horse manure and stale urine. Smashed wooden boxes, broken furniture and torn mattresses were piled along the sides of the alley. Above him in the darkness, clothes hung on lines stretching across the alley. There was a moon, but it was out of sight somewhere behind the buildings.

Longarm suddenly halted.

"I didn't tell you to stop."

Longarm felt the barrel dig deeper into his back.

"Keep moving!"

"What's this all about, Barton?"

The man laughed shortly. "You mean you don't know?"

Slowly, Longarm turned to face Barton. He was holding an oversized Navy Colt and looked as if he knew how to handle it.

"This is crazy, Barton," Longarm told him reasonably. "I don't have anything on you."

"Not yet you don't. Not until Ned Larson shows up. Now turn around and keep going."

Longarm started to turn, then ducked swiftly down on one knee and swung up his right arm, slapping the big Colt aside. It detonated, sending a round whistling past Longarm's shoulder. He grabbed the Colt's long barrel and twisted it violently out of Barton's grasp.

Barton turned and ran.

Longarm aimed and fired quickly, intending to catch the man low. But he was unfamiliar with the big revolver's balance. The round whined off the alley wall. He fired again. This round slammed Barton forward onto the alley floor. He skidded facedown a good distance over the slick manure before coming to a halt.

When Longarm reached him and flung him over onto his back, he saw the gaping exit wound in his chest and swore. He had found the inside man, sure enough. He hadn't needed Ned Larson, after all—only the threat of him. But he wished Barton could still talk. Longarm had some questions that needed answering.

Shouts came from the mouth of the alley. A crowd had gathered and a constable, billy club in hand, was hurrying toward him. Longarm straightened up and reached for his wallet.

"Why, Longarm!" Amber exclaimed, pulling open the door to her apartment. "I thought you'd decided not to come."

"Your invite still good?" he asked.

"Why, of course! You know that. Get in here!"

Longarm stepped into the apartment. Amber closed the door and leaned her back against it. "Well, now, you're here at last. That's what counts."

"You look good enough to eat."

"Promise?"

She was wearing a frilly nightdress, cut low enough for him to glimpse generous portions of her creamy breasts. Her hair was combed out, its gleaming glossy black surface an effective contrast to the bottle-green of her nightdress.

He put down his carpetbag and looked around.

The gleaming waxed floors were covered with midnight-black rugs, while the apartment itself was a study in various shades of red—from pink to fire-engine red. The wallpaper was light pink as were the floor-length drapes. The couch and parlor chairs were upholstered in red brocade. The tea table was a highly polished black lacquer. And to add the final, garish touch, the shades on all the gas lamps were bright red, casting a lurid glow over the walls and the white ceiling.

"Nice," he said, "but maybe a mite . . . garish. Reminds me of a very expensive parlor house. Maybe too expensive for a working man like myself."

She smiled warmly. "For you, Longarm, it's on the house."

He stepped toward her. She opened her arms. He moved into them and kissed her. She held him close, her lips opening, her tongue probing with a robust wantonness only she could command. He swept her up in his arms and with her directing him, carried her into the bedroom. Walk-in closets covered the walls on both sides of the bed, their doors faced with mirrors. The bed was enormous and over it stretched an enormous silk canopy. The pink satin coverlet had been thrown back, revealing black silk sheets.

This last touch caused Longarm to laugh out loud as he dumped Amber onto the bed. "You pulled out all the stops, Amber. Yessir, this is some parlor house you got here."

"I thought you'd like it." She winked mischievously.

Peeling out of her nightdress, she slipped quickly under the covers and watched as Longarm shrugged out of his frock coat and draped his cross-draw rig over the back of a chair.

"You going to tell me what happened, Longarm? I mean, you woke me out of a sound sleep. Why are you so late? The Bennington isn't that far."

"Later, Amber. First things first."

Longarm folded his frock coat onto the throw rug beside the bed, then folded his vest carefully and let it fall onto the coat, careful to keep the vest pockets on top. Amber got to her knees on the bed behind him, reached over his shoulders and unbuttoned his shirt, and pulled it off. He peeled down his pants and long johns, then scooted up on the bed until his back rested against the headboard. With a deep, contented sigh, Amber crawled into his arms and rested her head on his chest.

"You going to tell me now what happened?" she asked.

"Sure. That gent you pointed out to me downstairs. Barton. He tried to kill me."

Amber pushed away and stared at him, eyes wide. "My God," she exclaimed. "What happened?"

He grinned. "Can't you tell? I'm still here, ain't I?"

She tucked her head under his chin again and snuggled close. "Oh, I'm so glad," she said. "Did you . . . catch him?"

"He's in the lockup now. I'll be taking him to Denver with me in the morning. Looks like my visit to Pueblo won't last all that long."

"Did . . . did he say anything?"

"Like what?"

"I mean did he admit he was the one who tipped off Ned Larson and those others about the silver shipment?"

"Not yet. But he will. He works in the smelter. He had the opportunity. And he knows Ned Larson. Who else could have been the tipster? I'll get a chance to grill him on the train ride back to Denver. After all," he concluded, squeezing her gently, "I was tired and there was someone I wanted to see. Real bad."

"But what about Ned Larson?"

"If he shows up, Amber, I'm counting on you

to alert the authorities—and maybe keep him around so we can pick him up."

"That's not a very pleasant assignment, Custis."

"Can I count on you, Amber?"

She sighed. "I'll think about it."

She lifted her face to his. He bent and kissed her. Then he rolled gently over onto her. Murmuring in rapt appreciation, Amber tightened her arms about his neck and spread her thighs for him.

Knowing what he did, however, it was difficult for Longarm to perform.

Amber was all concern and tenderness, however, and through pure witchery managed to firm him up at last, enabling him to enter her. That was when he saw one of the mirrored doors beside the bed shift as someone stepped out into the bedroom. Longarm flung himself off Amber. A powerful detonation shook the room. Amber screamed. Longarm kept on rolling across the bed. A second round punched into a pillow and filled the air with feathers. He dropped off the bed as another shot slammed into the mattress inches from his head.

Digging the derringer out of his vest pocket, he grabbed the bed frame and swung himself under the bed. He saw his would-be assassin's boots tramping around to the other side of the bed to get at him. Spinning himself around on the highly polished floor, Longarm reached up, grabbed the bed's frame, and pulled his head and shoulders out from under the foot of the bed.

Looking up, he saw Wes Longbranch's back. The man spun about. The derringer in Longarm's hand barked. The first bullet caught Longbranch squarely in the center of his yellow vest, the second sliced up through his jaw, exploding out the back of his head. Gurgling unpleasantly, Longbranch dropped his gun and crumpled to the floor.

"Longarm . . . !"

He scrambled to his feet. Still on the bed, Amber was flat on her back, a puckered hole in her side. The sheets under her rippled from the steady rush of blood coming from the exit wound.

"I been hit," she said, her breathing shallow, hurried. "Wes . . . that stupid bastard . . . he hit me!"

Lifting her gently to inspect the exit wound, he realized her injuries were mortal. Against the black sheets, her stark pallor was frightening. He placed a pillow under her head.

"Will you forgive me, Custis?"

"For sending Barton after me?"

She nodded.

"I'll bet that was Wes's idea."

"Yes, Custis . . . it was."

"Why did he want Barton to kill me?"

"Wes . . . been using Barton . . . tip off other shipments . . . doing this for years."

"He works at the smelter, too?"

She nodded feebly. "Yes . . ."

It was what Longarm had figured. And Wes

had been in here with her when Longarm knocked. Her surprise when she opened the door to see him standing there had told him that. It was not difficult to guess why they had not expected him.

"Lay back, Amber. I'll get a doctor."

"No, please! Stay with me. A doc ain't goin' to help me now."

He wanted to contradict her, to assure her that she was going to be just fine. Only he couldn't get the words out. She reached out to him. He took her hand. It's lack of warmth chilled him.

"It was business, Custis," she gasped, "just business...nothin' personal. Wes, he threatened...take Lucky Lady...from me."

"Rest easy, Amber."

"No hard feelings?"

"For sure, Amber. No hard feelings."

She smiled and closed her eyes. "You... always was a gentleman, Custis."

Her pale face seemed to sink into the black pillow. He waited a moment, until he felt the marble coldness of her hand chilling him. He lay her hand gently down on the satin sheet, dressed quickly, and stepping over Longbranch's body, hurried from the apartment.

It was after the supper hour, and Longarm and Billy Vail were sharing a bottle of Maryland rye. Billy Vail had come over to the Windsor's bar especially to see Longarm. Vail had some news for him, apparently, but so far had kept it to himself. Meanwhile, Longarm finished recounting in much greater detail than before the events leading up to Amber's death and that of her partner.

Billy Vail leaned back in the plush booth and regarded Longarm quizzically. "Why do you think Longbranch tried to kill you?"

"He overheard me, like I knew he would. He thought Barton was still alive. With me dead, he could use his influence to quash any further investigation and possibly get Barton off. He had no choice but to step out of that closet and try to kill me."

Vail shook his head. "You sure as hell played that one close to the vest."

Longarm lit his second cheroot.

"How did you know Amber had tipped off Barton?"

"When I confronted Barton in the alley, he mentioned Ned Larson showing up in Pueblo to finger him. The only one I had suggested that possibility to was Amber."

Billy shook his head. "Back stabber."

"Go easy on her. Like she said, it was only business. She put great store by that saloon, and her apartment above it. It was the biggest, silliest thing in her life. She couldn't let Longbranch take it from her."

"Anyway, the authorities in Pueblo are damned pleased, Custis. They had no idea Longbranch was behind the petty thefts and heists that had been driving them crazy for years. Hell, they were thinking seriously of making him head honcho.

Longarm refilled their glasses.

"Glad to have you back, Custis," Vail said warmly. "Until I got that telegram from Pueblo, I thought maybe Larson had gotten his hooks into you."

"He came close."

"You wondering why I came over?"

"I figured you'd tell me when you were ready."

"I got a telegram from the town marshal in Bonanza, that mining town you mentioned."

"Gunnison?"

"That's him."

"What's he want?"

"Seems a few days ago some prospectors looking for copper ore found some. They found something else, too. They found Ned Larson."

Longarm leaned close. He had told Billy Vail only that he had lost Ned Larson in the mountains, then headed south on his own to Pueblo. "You mean they found his body?"

"He's alive. Sort of. Missing most of his left arm, with gangrene eating away what's left. And out of his head. Crazy as a loon is how Gunnison put it. It was a fairly long telegram. He says they're goin' to try him for the killing of that sidekick of yours and the hostler he clubbed to death when he entered the livery to get his horse. Gunnison wanted to know if we had any objection."

"What did you tell him?"

"Sent the telegram before I came over here. Told him to go right ahead and try the bastard."

"Any doubt about the verdict?"

Vail smiled. "I wouldn't think so. But if the rope don't get him, the gangrene will."

Longarm leaned back in the booth and glanced around him at the hotel's bar. He had planned to go into the back room later and deal himself into a quiet game of poker. But now he wasn't thinking of cards. He was thinking of a crazed, mad-dog killer stinking of putrefaction mounting a scaffold—and of the long, sad train of his victims. Stella Rooney, Santos, the kid, and all the others.

He wanted another drink. And after that, he knew, he would want still another. He looked wearily across the table at Billy Vail. "Stay a while, Billy. I think maybe I'm going to need some help tonight getting back to my room."

Understanding gleamed in Vail's shrewd eyes. "Sure thing, Custis. My pleasure."

Longarm reached for the Maryland rye.

Watch for

LONGARM AND THE HANGMAN'S NOOSE

One hundred twenty-fifth in the bold
LONGARM series from Jove

coming in May!

LONGARM

Explore the exciting Old West with
one of the men who made it wild!